The gentle tap-tap at her door broke her concentration

Jewel frowned. The knock sounded too damn familiar. The fact that she now recognized it as Taye's bid for entry into her dressing room—and that it sent her heart into a spin—was ridiculous!

Without asking who it was, she finished wiping off her makeup and flung open the door. Taye stepped in, closed it and simply stood and watched her. Jewel glared at her visitor, not sure where to start, her careful analysis of the situation suddenly evaporating.

What should I do? Play a role or play it out for real? However she didn't have time to speak, and didn't resist when she saw the flicker of desire in his eyes and felt his grip on her upper arms as he swept her flush against his chest.

"Everyone's gone," he murmured.

"Why did you come here?" she groaned against his shirt, knowing she had lost her battle of wills.

"Thought you might need a little more coaching."

Books by Anita Bunkley

Kimani Romance

Suite Embrace
Suite Temptation
Spotlight on Desire

ANITA BUNKLEY

is an author of seven successful mainstream novels and three novellas. A member of the Texas Institute of Letters and an NAACP Image Award nominee, she lives in Houston, Texas, with her husband, Crawford.

An avid reader all of her life, she was inspired to begin her writing career while researching the lives of interesting African-American women whose stories had not been told. A strong romantic theme has always been at the center of her novels and now she is enjoying writing true romance for her many fans.

Spotlight on *Desire*

Anita Bunkley

KIMANI™
ROMANCE

To my husband, Crawford, with love.

KIMANI PRESS™

ISBN-13: 978-0-373-86116-3

Recycling programs
for this product may
not exist in your area.

SPOTLIGHT ON DESIRE

Dear Reader,

Turn off the TV and enter the soap-opera world of Jewel Blaine, the sexy lead actress on *The Proud and the Passionate,* as she falls under the spell of her handsome director, Taye Elliott.

Jewel has risen to the top of her game by playing and living by a strict set of rules, but once Taye steps onto the set, her code to live by is quickly forgotten.

The fast-paced world of daytime television is the perfect medium for Taye—a stuntman turned director who has a lot to prove and a serious secret to hide. But as you know, Hollywood is not a place where secrets stay hidden for very long. As Jewel and Taye dodge prying eyes, they soon discover that there is no escaping the spotlight that shines on their emerging love.

Enjoy! If you want to drop me a line, please e-mail me at arbun@sbcglobal.net.

Read with love!

Anita Bunkley

Chapter 1

Galveston Island

"Come home with me, baby. Tonight."

"You know that's impossible."

"Nothing's impossible, Caprice. Not if you want it badly enough, and if you loved me half as much as you say you do, you'd leave this island tonight and come home."

"But, Darin...we can't return to Elm Valley together. Think of the scandal. It'll be better if you go ahead, and then I show up. I've got too much..."

"Cut!" A voice burst from the dark edges of the brightly lit patch of beach. Although the sun had set more than two hours ago, dissolving into Galveston Bay like a ball of liquid gold, huge overhead lights flooded the shoreline and created an island of activity in the otherwise-deserted cove.

Immediately, a fussy wardrobe attendant rushed onto the set and wrapped a thick white robe around Jewel Blaine, who smiled her thanks and closed it over her tiny gold bikini. The actress who played Caprice Desmond on *The Proud and the Passionate* (*P & P*) was petite, dark haired and flamboyantly attractive. At thirty-two, she had starred in the groundbreaking African-American soap opera since it debuted on TV five years ago.

Now, Jewel tilted her head, lowered her chin, widened her luminous brown eyes and spun around to face Brad Fortune, the man who called the shots on the set of *P & P*.

If we have to stay here all night to get it right, we will, she vowed.

As lead actress, Jewel felt personally responsible for the success of each episode and during her tenure on the daytime drama had won two Daytime Emmys, a BET Achievement Award, NAACP Image Award and many critical reviews.

Brad Fortune stopped less than a foot from where Jewel was standing, placed a slender hand on his right hip and narrowed his aquamarine eyes at his star, giving her one of his trademark extended moments. A confirmed bachelor who enjoyed the companionship of a male live-in friend, Brad possessed an instinctive awareness of his actors' needs and used this insight to gain their respect and trust. With twenty years in daytime television, he was a talented man who knew what audiences wanted and made sure his cast delivered.

Now, the sound of waves lapping at the sandy shore and the rustle of palm fronds filled the night air as everyone waited in respectful silence for Brad to speak. "Not quite enough confliction, Jewel," he said, his high-pitched voice lower than usual, his tone resolute. He swept a stray clump of reddish-brown hair back into his ponytail, cocked his head to one side and moved nearer to his star. "Infuse more worry into that line. Give me regret, some guilt. But hold firm! Remember, Caprice led Darin to believe that she'd do *anything* for him. *Anything.* And now she's reneging on her promise to go home with him. She's gotta sound conflicted. Understand?"

Jewel nodded. Brad was a pro, knew what he was after and she trusted him completely. No way would he put film in the can unless he believed the scene was the best that both he and his actors could deliver.

"Right, Brad," Sonny Burton interjected. "I agree completely." Nineteen years older than Jewel, Sonny Burton was well cast as Darin Saintclare, her mature on-screen lover. When CBC, the network that owned *P & P*, first lured handsome, charismatic Sonny Burton away from his popular daytime talk show to become a major black soap star, his national audience had cheered the decision. He was sexy and suave, with a fan of gray at his temples, a generous, welcoming smile and an easygoing style that contrasted sharply with Jewel's methodically organized approach to her work. However, despite their differences, the two stars created magical on-screen chemistry that drove their fans wild and, so far, pleased the executives at CBC.

Sonny cleared his throat, eyes shining with resolve, clearly wanting to please his director. "I know exactly what you're after. You want a real sense of Caprice pulling back from Darin, but at the same time…"

"Not overly dramatic. Right?" Jewel finished her costar's remark. "Caprice *wants* Darin, but she's afraid of how she'll be viewed by the nosy busybodies of Elm Valley if she gives in and returns home too soon."

"Exactly! Keep the relationship on target but slightly off balance. Jewel, you sure know your girl Caprice," Brad concurred, blessing Jewel with an appreciative smile. "Caprice might love Darin, but she's got to look out for herself, too."

Jewel winked at Sonny, giving him a conspiratorial nod of approval. During the past five years, the on-screen couple had fine-tuned their relationship until it rolled along like raindrops slipping down a windowpane. And even when sticky issues arose on the set, Sonny always had her back and she protected his.

"Caprice can't come off as too regretful," Jewel went on, clarifying her character's motivation. "She's got her pride, you know?"

"Fine, fine," Brad stated with a flip of his wrist as he turned around. "We all love Caprice as much as you do. Showing a little hesitant spunk in this scene is totally within character." A beat. "Okay, let's take it from the top, people," Brad called over his shoulder as he walked out of camera range. However, before clearing the illuminated set, he stopped abruptly and spun around, his blue-green eyes wide with shock. His mouth opened, shut and then opened again. "Damn!" he shouted, reeling backward and stumbling to a half fall. Braced on his knees, he groped for words. "I…I feel… Oh my God!" He slammed both hands, palms flat, against his chest and emitted a startling howl.

Shana Dane, the makeup artist whose job it was to keep the cast glossy-photo perfect, tossed her tray of brushes, sponges and cosmetics to the ground and rushed toward Brad, followed closely by Karen Adams, the second-tier segment producer.

"Brad! What's wrong?" Shana shouted, watching in horror as he collapsed on the sand.

Fred Warner, the executive producer of *P & P,* who had flown in from Los Angeles that morning to check on progress at the location shoot, jostled Shana and Karen aside to kneel over the fallen man.

"Call an ambulance! Somebody call 911!" Fred shouted frantically, cradling Brad's head on his lap.

"Doing it now," Sonny yelled, fumbling with a cell phone that he'd snatched from his pants pocket. He gave the emergency responder directions to their isolated location, unable to tell them more than someone had collapsed in pain and to get there as quickly as possible.

"Brad, Brad. What is it?" Fred urged, slipping an arm beneath Brad's shoulders to tilt the director closer. He pressed his ear to Brad's lips.

"I dunno," Brad managed to whisper. "Got hit with a terrible pain. Here, in my…" Brad's voice faded as his fingers groped the front of his shirt.

"Hold on, Brad! Hold on," Jewel urged, dropping to her knees next to Fred.

Sonny jammed his phone back into his pocket and crouched beside Jewel, his shoulder wedged tightly against hers. Jewel grabbed one of Brad's hands and squeezed it hard, scrunching even closer to urgently whisper, "Brad! Look at me! Open your eyes. Hold on! Hold on! Help is coming."

Brad's eyes fluttered open and then closed very quickly, as if trying to focus on Jewel took too much of his energy. His pale face was slick with perspiration, his lips blue and unmoving, his slim body as rigidly immobile as a mannequin's.

When he shuddered jerkily beneath Jewel's touch, she felt a jolt of hope.

"Brad! Brad! Don't you dare give up," she shouted over the shocked murmurs of the horrified cast and crew. Brad jerked wildly again. His legs shot upward, his arms flew out to the side and his head lolled from side to side before he went still.

"Where's the doctor? The ambulance? Dammit! We need some help!" Jewel shouted, her words threaded with terror. She gripped Brad's hand and pressed it hard against her lips, kissing the edge of his palm as she tamped the fingertips of her right hand down against his temple. Looking over at Sonny, a frown etched shadows on her face. "This is bad, Sonny." Her voice trembled. "I can't find a pulse. I think Brad is dead."

Chapter 2

The lobby of Tinsel Town Theater in Fox Hills Mall was crammed with die-hard devotees of action/slasher movies who had come out for the premier of *Terror Train 4*. After viewing the latest installment in the cultlike series, they were milling around, clutching rolled-up posters, stacks of DVDs and commemorative T-shirts to be signed by the stars.

"*Terror Train 4* kicked some serious butt," a short Hispanic boy with long black hair said as he shoved a DVD at Taye Elliott.

Taye eyed the square plastic case with interest, but did not take it from the guy. Instead, he rotated one shoulder in a noncommittal manner. "Sorry to disappoint, but I'm not one of the actors," he said. "I'm the director." He cocked his head toward the outer edge of the lobby where two men and two women sat high on a riser, behind a table draped with gold velvet. "The autographs you want are over there."

The long-haired boy mugged disinterest and gave Taye a flickering roll of his eyes. "Yeah? But you say you're the director, huh?"

"Yep. That's right."

"Hey, that's still cool, man. Gimme your autograph, too."

Taye felt a brief ripple of pleasure flare as he took out the black Sharpie pen he always carried and signed his name on the boy's DVD.

"You directed all of 'em?" the young man asked.

"All four films," Taye conceded with a touch of pride.

"That means you directed that wild chase scene on that bomb-rigged bridge in *Terror Train 2?*"

"Yep. I sure did."

"*Loved* it. The bomb! Hey, but I loved number four, too! The best so far, I think."

"Thanks. Glad you enjoyed it," Taye replied, appreciating the comment and impressed that the boy concurred with Taye: *Terror Train 4* was his best directorial work so far. After having worked as stunt man for fifteen years, he ought to know what made a memorable action film. The *Terror Train* series had given him the opportunity to prove what he could do and even though the series went straight to DVD and would never hit theaters nationwide, it created a solid base of followers and pulled in substantial international sales.

"Is it true? Is this the last *Terror Train* movie?" the fan asked, sounding genuinely distressed.

"Yeah. This is it for the series."

"Damn, man. That sucks," the boy grumbled. "Why somethin' this great gotta end?"

Taye offered a noncommittal lift of his eyebrows as the same question hung in his mind, feeling as agitated and frustrated as the boy. However, he understood how the industry worked: Taye was only a director. The money people held all the power. And without funding, there couldn't be a deal. "Even good things gotta end sometime, you know?" he finally stated.

"I guess," the boy grudgingly remarked, adding, "Stay cool."

"Sure will," Taye agreed, reaching up to slap palms with the guy, who slipped off into the crush of people clumped around the table where the real stars of the movie busily greeted fans.

Moving to a quieter spot in the lobby, Taye leaned against a wall and watched the animated audience move past, liking what he saw: young males in sports-branded clothing, slouch jeans, T-shirts and baseball caps. Girls in tight T-shirts, lots of jewelry, low-rise jeans and flip-flops on their feet. They were white, African American, Asian, Hispanic. Mostly young, but there was also a substantial number of graying baby boomers visible in the crowd.

A fair-skinned woman with dyed blond hair, accompanied by a bearded guy who looked stoned, stopped in front of Taye, breaking into his assessment of the audience. "You look better in person," she bluntly assessed, blue eyes boring into Taye.

Taye snapped alert and stared at her. "What?"

She repeated her comment, even more emphatically the second time.

"Oh? Well, sorry," he said. "*I* wasn't in the movie."

"I know you weren't, but you're a movie star, right?"

He chuckled low in his throat. "Nope. Got the wrong man. Sorry, I'm not an actor."

"But I've seen you somewhere. I know I have," she insisted, cracking gum that bounced from one side of her mouth to the other while intently studying Taye. "I got it! Read about you on Hollywood WebWatch. You're the stunt man who doubles for all those big stars."

"Used to," Taye conceded with an edge of defiance, not particularly interested in talking about those days.

A pause. "Mario Van Peebles in *Downtown Killer,* right?" the woman blurted with glee.

Surprised to have this bit of trivia thrown at him, Taye simply nodded.

"And that was the movie where an extra got killed in a car chase and you got hurt real bad, wasn't it?"

A stream of air slipped from between Taye's lips as he inclined his head in surrender. "You got it right," he admitted, realizing that he should never underestimate how closely the public followed movies, movie stars and all the peripherals connected to the industry. With all the blogs and Web sites and Internet chats going on 24/7, it was easy to find obscure details about actors, doubles, scene sequences, writers and obviously former stunt people like himself.

The woman bobbed her head up and down, sending her halo of blond hair into a frizzy dance. "I *knew* I was right. Tore up your back and now you direct *Terror Train* films."

"A lot safer line of work," Taye offered, giving her a playful thumbs-up.

"Yeah…well, you still got that stuntman body." She raked Taye with an appreciative glance that lingered at his horseshoe-shaped belt buckle and then swept down to his black ostrich-skin boots. She ran her tongue over cherry-red lips and sighed.

Suppressing a laugh, Taye raised both hands, palms up, as if to deflect the uninvited compliment. "Even a director's gotta keep in shape, you know?"

"Hey, that's cool. The ladies love a man who's tight…on and off the screen." She shot an appraising look at her bearded companion, gave up an easy snicker and then headed out into the mall.

Taye laughed aloud, not completely surprised that he'd been mistaken for an actor. He'd stunt doubled for Mario, Will, Wesley and even Denzel in dozens of movies before injuring his back in that rollover crash nearly four years ago. With his career in stunt work compromised, he'd decided to try his hand at directing and had taken on the *Terror Train* series as soon as it was offered. Shifting from in front of the camera to behind it had been a risky move, but Taye had never been one to shy away from risks. And while accumulating his directing credentials, he'd also formed valuable alliances with important industry people who were proving to be very helpful. He already had a new project lined up that presented quite a challenge.

When the movie crowd thinned, Taye went over to the stars, thanked them for coming out to promote the film and then headed to the mall parking lot. He got into his dark green Hummer truck, fastened his seat belt and glanced into the side-view mirror, catching his reflection while recalling the blond woman's remarks.

In Hollywood, image was everything and although Taye no longer stunt doubled for handsome A-list actors, he enjoyed walking into a room and causing a stir, especially among women, even though he'd sworn off all but the most casual of relationships since ending his marriage nearly two years ago.

Chapter 3

Jewel could hardly believe that Brad Fortune was gone, struck down by a massive heart attack due to a long-standing heart condition. *And it happened so fast,* she sadly recalled as she braked at a red light and scanned the block until she saw Bon Ami, the restaurant where she was meeting Fred Warner for lunch.

Sitting at the corner of Rodeo Drive and Beverly Lane, her thoughts remained on Brad. She, along with everyone connected with *The Proud and the Passionate,* remained stunned by the loss of their beloved director. Brad had appeared to be in perfect health, with the energy and physique of a much younger man. However, he had vigorously protected his private life, so it should not have come as a surprise that he'd kept his illness a secret.

Jewel missed him terribly. They had clicked the first day on the set when, at the end of the shoot, they'd hunkered down in her dressing room with a bottle of Cristal champagne to toast the launch of the show. They'd gotten slightly drunk, bared their souls about their hopes and dreams and goals for their careers and bonded in a special way. Brad had made it easy for Jewel to display the raw emotion that her role as Caprice Desmond demanded. With him, she'd been able to lose herself in her character and give her heart and soul to the camera without inhibition or self-conscious worry.

A swell of sorrow came over Jewel, but she refused to let it build.

No one will ever replace Brad, she sadly mused. *But he's dead and as difficult as that is to accept, I have to press on. I just hope to God that whoever steps in measures up to the standards Brad set.*

After handing her silver Lexus sedan over to the parking attendant, Jewel stepped out onto the sidewalk and glanced around. The trendy eatery on Rodeo Drive was a convenient meeting place for Jewel and Fred, as it was halfway between his home in Beverly Hills and her house in Brentwood. The white stone, multiterraced building was buzzing with activity on all three levels, packed with impeccably dressed people as well as tourists in casual clothing, cameras primed to snap photos of someone famous.

Jewel gave her gem-studded jeans a tug, fluttered the wide sleeves of her gauzy black top and touched her Chanel wraparound sunglasses for security, bracing for the paparazzi that she had no doubt were lurking nearby. She swept her eyes over the people sitting at the linen-draped tables nibbling zero-calorie endive-arugula salads and drinking pastel vitamin waters. She saw familiar faces and strangers, too. And in her mind's eye she also saw fans, the people who appreciated her work, followed her career and were eagerly awaiting the conclusion of the cliffhanger story line that had been so abruptly interrupted by Brad's untimely death.

Just as she'd suspected, a photographer rushed over and squatted down in front of her, initiating his usual clamor for a photo. She obliged, fluffing up her loose curly hair, striking a flirty, sexy pose with both hands on her hips and easing a pouty smile onto her lips. Jewel grinned and waved at the camera as well as at the curious onlookers who began moving forward, eager to see saucy Caprice Desmond—the character she loved to play and the public loved to follow—in the flesh. While maintaining her public-perfect pose, Jewel graciously accepted pens, pencils and pieces of paper that were thrust at her, happy to scribble "Love, Caprice" on each one.

When the Bon Ami hostess managed to push through the crowd to escort Jewel to her table, Jewel laughingly called out, "No more autographs. I'd like to eat lunch now, okay?" The crowd fell back, the photographer stood. With a quick wave, Jewel made her exit and walked up a short flight of steps to the outdoor patio where Fred was waiting, BlackBerry handheld pressed to his ear, a glass of white wine nearby.

Jewel gave Fred an airbrushed kiss before sitting.

"Just be a sec," he told her, index finger raised.

"Take your time," Jewel whispered in a breathy voice, before asking the server to bring her a Perrier water and lime. She settled into the white wrought-iron chair across from her producer and then glanced down at the street-level entry to the restaurant. People were milling around, waiting for their cars and chatting before saying goodbye.

Scanning the crowd, she was struck by the design on the back of a man's shirt. The swirling collage of red, blue, yellow and green came together in what looked like an eagle, wings spread. It seemed oddly familiar. The man wearing it was talking to a parking valet and gesturing with his hands. Jewel tilted forward to get a closer look, but he disappeared inside the restaurant, so she put it out of her mind.

Some struggling actor, she decided. *Hanging around the restaurant, hoping to get the attention of a director or a casting agent.* She knew his type. Los Angeles was full of men and women like him—obsessed with creating a splashy impression, so they'd be noticed and, hopefully, offered a movie role. *He's probably a menswear salesman wearing a store sample,* she mused, ripping her gaze from the street below just as Fred finished his call and the server placed her water on the table.

"So, tell me. Who's our new director? I'm so ready to get back to work." Jewel plunged right in, taking a sip of her drink.

Fred Warner slipped his handheld into the inside pocket of his beige linen suit and adjusted his tan silk tie. "Yeah, well, everyone is." He sat back, lowered his chin and gave Jewel a look that lasted long enough to let his silence send a message of reassurance. Fred Warner, executive producer of *The Proud and the Passionate,* was fifty-two years old, two inches shy of six feet tall and startlingly corporate in both appearance and demeanor. His hair was silver, full and impeccably styled. His jewelry was real, understated and tasteful. He wore suits crafted by European designers and hand-made monogrammed shirts and insisted on being chauffeured around town in a white Bentley luxury car that reflected his status as a man with power and money.

"The network has decided to bring in Taye Elliott. He'll fill in as executive director to take us through May sweeps."

"Hmm, I don't know him. What's he done?" Jewel asked.

"New to daytime but comes with good credentials," Fred replied.

"Yeah? Tell me more."

"Youngish…well, younger than Brad. Midthirties. Divorced. No kids…he made a point of informing us of that. Said he's free to work round the clock, if we need him."

"Mmm-hmm. But what's he been doing, if not daytime?" Jewel asked, eager for the professional credentials of the man she'd start working with on Monday. "Lifetime movies? Hallmark? A&E?"

"Nope. Nothing like that." Fred tasted his wine, a silver eyebrow arched. "Ever heard of the *Terror Train* series?"

Jewel shook her head, confused. "No…they sound like teenage action/slasher flicks."

Fred started to reply but stopped when the waiter arrived to take their order. He glanced at Jewel, who shook her head. Suddenly, eating was the last thing on her mind.

"We'll order later," Fred advised the young man, turning back to Jewel. "Basically, you're pretty much on target. Action movies have been Taye Elliott's forte. He did stunt double work for a lot of A-list actors…Wesley Snipes, Denzel, Will Smith."

"Oh, he's black?" Jewel commented, impressed. She could count on one hand the number of African Americans behind the camera in daytime television. This guy must be pretty damn good to have been tapped for a job like this. Suddenly, she was more eager than ever to meet him.

"Right. He doubled for Mario in that scene where he jumps off the roof of that skyscraper in *The First Real War.* Fantastic work. He won the award for best action movie star at the World Stunt Awards. Did you see that movie?"

Jewel shook her head no.

"Anyway," Fred continued, "a few years back, Taye injured his spine in a car crash, decided to give up stunt work and try his hand at directing. Took on the *Terror Train* series…independently financed films that went straight to DVD." Fred fiddled with a gold cuff link shaped like a half-moon, eyes locked on Jewel. "He did a heck of a job, impressed his producers and started making noise in circles that count."

Even though Jewel trusted Fred and wanted to share his enthusiasm for this unknown former stuntman turned director, an alarming sense of apprehension began to rise. Her mind jumped ahead to visions of Taye cursing at his actors, corralling them onto the set like cattle on the range and of tough-guy talk in a brusque commando style.

"I don't get it," Jewel said, apprehension evident. "How can an action-hero stuntman replace a classy guy like Brad Fortune?"

"Former stuntman," Fred deadpanned his response, the tip of his tongue pressed to his lower lip.

"Okay, former stuntman," Jewel conceded, struggling to control her sense of unease, but wanting to hear the network's rationale for going in this direction. "What am I missing, Fred? What qualifies Elliott to direct a soap opera?"

Hand raised, Fred cautioned patience. "I hear you, Jewel, and I understand your concern, but I really do think Taye Elliott will be a good fit. He'll bring a fresh approach to the show and, hopefully, help us lock down that young demographic that's been slipping. Daytime drama won't be a problem for him. He's used to fast-paced work and story lines that use recurring characters. He's got a good track record…comes in on time, under budget and delivers tightly controlled, effective scenes. I have to believe he can do the job. I've screened every movie he's directed and I gotta say, they might be action films, but they have beautifully crafted love scenes, too. They're huge hits with his target audience.…"

"Which is?" Jewel sullenly interrupted, too concerned with how this new director would affect her work to mask her growing irritation.

"Youth. Viewers between eighteen and thirty. The market we've *got* to go after hard…and hold on to. We're heading into May sweeps with ratings that have been slipping a point a week. We're counting on Taye to reverse that trend."

"And I know what the problem is," Jewel grudgingly concurred. "*Down for Love*'s debut in January."

"Exactly. *DFL* is kickin' our butts, pulling all the younger viewers, and if we don't catch up soon, we may not survive this ratings war."

"And you think Taye Elliott is the savior who will snatch that audience away from *DFL?*"

"I do. I think he's precisely what we need right now." Fred sounded confident, even though a new frown line deepened on his slightly freckled forehead.

"In theory, that sounds good, but it won't be easy for him to step in, pick up the *P & P* story lines and pull off a winning sweeps finale. This is April, Fred. There's not much time. This is gonna be rough on everyone."

Fred rounded his lips over obviously capped teeth and shifted forward in his seat. "I know, Jewel. That's why I want you to meet him, get to know him before you start working together. You can help smooth out his introduction. Make him feel comfortable, all right?"

Jewel didn't respond, wondering if she should take Fred up

on that. Certainly, she was dedicated to making *P & P* the top-rated daytime drama, but why stick out her neck to support a novice director? However, because the studio was firmly behind Taye, she had no choice but to agree to Fred's request.

Pulling in a slow breath, Jewel groped for a less-than-pessimistic mind-set, knowing she needed an attitude adjustment. "Fine. Fred, I'll do whatever I can to help Taye Elliott settle in and get his footing."

"I knew you'd feel that way. You're a real pro, Jewel, and Elliott will appreciate your cooperation."

"So, when do I meet him?"

Instead of responding, Fred shifted his focus above Jewel's head and made a calculating jerk with his chin. "Here he comes right now."

Jewel turned around in her seat, looked toward the entry and was shocked to see the man wearing the fancy black shirt walking toward her. He had a smugly confident expression on his face and was moving across the room with long, purposeful strides. *He looks entirely too self-satisfied,* Jewel observed, gripping the arm of her chair to steady herself when he stopped, looked down and said, "Ms. Blaine?"

In answer, she slowly dropped her chin, eyeing him from beneath thick lashes.

"I'm Taye Elliott." He offered her his hand.

Jewel stood up to take it and immediately two things clicked in her mind. First, his palm was dry and cool. Second, his fresh lemon-lime scent was making the muscles in her stomach tighten, freezing her greeting on her tongue.

Chapter 4

Gulping her surprise, Jewel floundered for a moment and then regained her voice. "Yes, I'm Jewel Blaine. Good to meet you, Taye." She squeezed his hand, quickly let it go and then sat down, struck by an irresistible urge to grin. He was one fine brother! Just the touch of his hand had rocked her, shaken her, made her go damp in her panties! And she was supposed to maintain a professional cool while following this man's direction? That was certainly going to be a challenge.

Keep it together, girl, she silently reprimanded. *Gotta play this one right. Can't act too glad to meet him.* Luckily, the waiter arrived to take their orders, interrupting the electrified lull, providing Jewel a chance to regain her composure.

Deciding on shrimp salads all around made it easy on the server and while Taye consulted with the young man on the wine, Jewel studied her new director's ruggedly appealing profile.

The tiny nicks and scars on the side of his face only added to his Alpha-male image. *Trophies from his stuntman days,* Jewel surmised, her eyes moving over his rich tan skin. He had sooty brown eyes that sloped gently at the edges in a lazy slant that sent serious bedroom signals. His jawline was severe, but rounded at the chin, softening an otherwise-tough-guy face. Flared nostrils capped a keen nose. Black curly hair that was slightly unruly, but still well-groomed. *I'd love to slip my little finger through that ringlet behind his ear,* Jewel impulsively mused, shifting her attention to the vintage Cartier watch on Taye's wrist. *The man's got good taste,* she allowed, moving on to assess his flamboyant shirt once more, realizing why it seemed familiar. Ralph Lauren. Last season. She'd seen it on the runway during Fashion Week in New York.

Fred Warner broke Jewel's mental trippin' with a jolt. "Jewel, I was telling Taye that you and the *P & P* cast are ready to get back before the cameras." He blinked at Jewel, clearly urging her to jump in and express her mutual delight with the studio's newest hire.

Getting Fred's message, Jewel locked eyes with Taye, who shot her a dazzling smile. Exhaling, she plunged ahead. "I agree completely," she hurried to say. "The cast is fired up and ready to get on with the show. And please, Taye, let me know if I can help in any way…as far as characters, motivation or backstory go."

"Thanks, I'm sure I'll need to take you up on that and I have to say…what an impossibly wonderful and complicated character you play, Jewel. Caprice Desmond is somethin' else."

"Yeah, she's a sister on a mission, all right," Jewel jokingly agreed. "And the more you get to know Caprice, the more you'll love her." Jewel gulped. *Damn! Why'd she say that?*

"I'm sure I will," Taye concurred in a melodious voice that initiated a warm pulse inside Jewel. She held very still as his attention slipped from her face to the gold chain settled in her cleavage and then back up to her lips.

Jewel resisted the urge to show him how amused she was by his obvious visual meandering. Clearing her throat, she adopted an all-about-business tone. "You'll find the cast easy to work with," she said. "No divas, neurotics or dual personalities among us. We're a pretty normal bunch, so don't be nervous."

"I won't be as long as you're around to keep things sane."

"I'm on the set every day, except most Fridays. If things do get crazy, and they can…or if stuff starts to unravel, I'll do what I can to help you sort it all out."

"I'm sure it won't take long for *everything* to fall into place," Taye replied with a self-assurance that made Jewel flinch.

Unable to hold back any longer, Jewel launched the question that had been uppermost in her mind since he sat down. "What got you interested in directing daytime drama? Are you a longtime soap fan?"

"Not at all," he quickly and laughingly confessed. "But I do appreciate the genre and I love a great romance. The *Terror Train* films incorporate romantic subplots with passionate, star-crossed lovers. They provide a nice respite from all the action…and encourage both the men and women to see the movies."

Sounds reasonable, Jewel thought, while not thoroughly convinced that Taye completely understood what he was getting into. "Okay, you like romance and action, but still…if your expertise is action flicks, isn't this a huge departure from the genre you're most comfortable with?" It was time to get real, get down to the essence of who Taye Elliott was and why he thought he could direct *The Proud and the Passionate*.

Settling back in his chair, Taye went calm, assessing Jewel with vaguely sensuous eyes. "This is how it happened," he started. "I guess I was in the right place at the right time and had the right vibes working for me. Like surviving an accidental collision that has positive results, you know?"

"Accident? Collision? No, sorry. I don't understand at all." Jewel tossed a questioning look at Fred, who mugged innocence and shrugged. *Did Taye just compare directing* P & P *to a car wreck? A crash? No surprise there.* With an obvious sigh of frustration, she launched her next zinger. "How exactly *did* you get in line to be *P & P*'s next director?"

Taye flashed Jewel a magnetic smile. "I'm happy to explain."

Jewel bent forward, anxious for the story behind this surprising development.

Taye squinted at Fred, appearing uneasy, confirming Jewel's suspicion that her question may have caught him off guard. "Well…you see," Taye began. "Richie Farral, who produced the action movies that I directed, is Arthur Platt's half brother."

"*The* Arthur Platt?" Jewel had to cut Taye off. "The former CEO of CBC?"

"Right. So, I was talking to Richie about my plans after *Terror Train,* and he mentioned his relationship with Arthur Platt."

Jewel went slack-jawed while listening to Taye, slightly annoyed by how casually he was tossing around the names of major players in the industry. Richie Farral was up there with Spielberg and Eastwood and Lucas. And Arthur Platt was the legendary founder of the network that carried her show, a hard-nosed billionaire rarely seen in public and not known to be a generous man.

"So I told Richie I was open for a change, you know? A project that would challenge me," Taye was saying as Jewel struggled to concentrate. "A few days later, Richie called to tell me that Platt had alerted him to this temporary gig for a director for a daytime drama, so I took a meeting with CBC and here I am."

Now, she was truly annoyed. "Oh, really? It was that easy?"

"Yep. Wasn't much more to it," Taye confessed.

The ring of pride in his snappy reply sent blood rushing into Jewel's head. A flicker of anger propelled her next comment. "So, *The Proud and the Passionate* is your test case? An experiment to gauge your ability to direct a daytime drama?"

Taye scoffed a laugh. "No, nothing like that."

"No, not at all," Fred jumped in in support of the studio's pick.

But Jewel wasn't about to let either of them off so easily. "Sounds like *P & P* is little more than a guinea-pig project as far as you're concerned," she threw at Taye, not particularly liking what she'd heard and letting her displeasure show. To her, the whole thing smacked of a good-old-boy hire—done quickly to fill a gap, with little thought to how such a snap decision might affect the cast.

Now, Fred Warner leaned low on one elbow, close to Jewel,

obviously concerned about where this exchange was headed. "Nothing like that is going on, Jewel. Taye's got what we…"

"Wait a minute, Fred," Taye interrupted, slicing the air at chest level with a sweep of one hand. "I can speak for myself. I'd like to clear up Ms. Blaine's concerns."

"All right with me. Have at it." Jewel sat back, ready to listen.

Turning to Jewel, Taye rounded his shoulders, gave her a quiet stare and then said, "You need to know that I'm a man who is constantly learning. Maybe that's why I went into stunt work in the first place. Every scene, every stunt, every movie was different and I like that, as well as the challenges that come with each new film. I view risky situations as opportunities to push myself, to see how far I can go with my talent and the talent of the actors. Daytime drama will expand my experience, diversify my body of work. I view every project as a collaborative effort to perfect a common creative vision."

"But what if the creative visions of the actor and the director are traveling separate paths?" Jewel tested, having no idea what his creative vision for *P & P* might be or if she'd share it once she knew. How could a hunky stunt guy whose head was filled with images of fiery action sequences and love scenes in the backs of race cars possibly grasp the nuanced passion, silky romance and complicated personal relationships that made up a daytime drama? *A long shot, at best,* Jewel decided.

"If there's disagreement, then we compromise, of course. It's all about working together to get the best footage in the can, isn't it?" Taye asked.

A short hesitation while Jewel considered his remark, thankful that at least his answer had a ring of sincerity. Compromise was good. Working together was vital and she had no choice but to cooperate fully with Taye. After all, she had legions of loyal fans and was committed to protecting her hard-won reputation as a dependable actress who never failed to deliver exactly what her fans expected. And, she reminded herself, Taye Elliott was only a temporary hire. She'd be at *P & P* long after he was gone.

Forcing a more rational attitude into play, she decided to give him the benefit of the doubt. "Good approach," she tossed back, a bit warmer. "You're absolutely right. We all want what's best for the show."

Taye sagged back in his seat, seemingly relieved to have passed that hurdle. "I've met with Lori, your head writer, and I'm up on the current relationships, but I could still use some help with the backstory on Caprice and Darin's long-standing love affair."

"Sure, it's very complicated. How can I help?" Jewel offered.

"I was wondering," Taye started, followed by a slight hesitation. "If it's not an imposition, think you, Sonny and I might squeeze in an hour or so tomorrow to go over a few areas of the current story line?"

In the lull that followed, Jewel calculated her answer. Should she agree? Demonstrate her willingness to help? Or let him know that Jewel Blaine had other things to do on Saturday than talk story line with her executive director? "Well, I don't know," she hedged, watching for his reaction.

"I know it's short notice and I'd hate to cut into your weekend," he rushed to add. "So, if you're busy, I understand. Just a thought...that maybe we could get a jump on Monday, but..."

Jewel's mind flipped to the weekend. For the first time in months, she had no public appearances, charity events, social engagements or a date with one of the devoted bachelors she partied with when she felt like hitting the club scene or going out for a quiet dinner. In fact, she'd been looking forward to a few days at home alone to catch up on fan mail or simply lounge by the pool before launching back into work on Monday. But did she really want Taye Elliott to know that?

"Saturday's not so good," she decided. "Really busy all morning and most of the afternoon." She swept her tongue over her teeth, appearing to be perplexed. "And I never work on Sundays if I can avoid it. That's *my* day...totally mine to relax, do nothing I don't feel like doing."

"I heard that," Taye agreed with a knowing smile. "We all need downtime. But what about later on Saturday? Maybe the three of us could talk over dinner?"

Startled by his persistence, Jewel inched one shoulder higher than the other in a subtle stall, thinking that one through.

Fred shot Jewel an impatient glance, which she interpreted as *It might be a good idea, Jewel,* while she was telling herself, *Don't push too hard, Mr. New-to-*P & P-*Director. I don't like to be crowded.*

Their shrimp salads arrived, temporarily letting her off the hook as they settled in to eat. During lunch, they discussed the shooting schedule leading into May sweeps and the kind of focus Fred wanted on the upcoming episodes.

An hour later, over dessert of pecan praline cheesecake, Jewel finally answered Taye. "Tell you what," she started. "Maybe I can squeeze in an hour or two tomorrow. Early evening. Can I call you later to set a time?"

"That'd be great," Taye replied with enthusiasm, handing Jewel his card, seeming pleased that his request might be accommodated.

"And I'll call Sonny. See if he can fit it in," Jewel offered, praying her costar would be available because meeting alone with Taye Elliott didn't seem like such a good idea. "Now, tell me how you see Caprice Desmond and Darin Saintclare's love story unfolding during sweeps," she asked, making a mental shift in the jumble of unanswered questions cascading through her mind.

Sitting back, Jewel listened with interest to the man whose presence was sending all the wrong signals. Whose eyes were undressing her. Whose cologne was stoking a pleasure point deep inside her core and whose voice was challenging her long-standing, never-to-be-broken rule: no romantic involvement with anyone connected with her career.

Chapter 5

Taye drove away from Bon Ami with both hands tensed on the steering wheel of his truck, as if holding on to it kept Jewel Blaine's image from slipping away too soon. Damn, she was hot! He could still feel her luminous brown eyes engaged with his, smell the delicate perfume that drifted from her beige-tan cleavage, hear the titillating chime of her voice in his ears. The heat of his reaction filled his gut, simmering there like hot coals banked to hold their warmth. Flushed with a strange sense of anticipation, he was not surprised that just thinking about her initiated the beginnings of an arousal that had no business existing and definitely no place to go.

She was more beautiful in person than she was on TV. Soft sable-brown hair, pulled back into a cascading upsweep of curls that created a sophisticated yet playful appearance. Smoky brown eyes that could flash with intelligence or simmer in sexy seduction. Skin like satiny sweet toffee—candy that he'd love to feel melting in his mouth. A diminutive powerhouse of a woman with gorgeous curves and the electric chemistry that put her slightly out of reach, even though her low-cut blouse had exposed sufficient cleavage to tease him, to dare him to try to shatter that proper-public image she presented to the world.

Taye smiled to himself. Jewel Blaine might not know much about him, but he sure knew a hell of a lot about her. Before their meeting today, he'd scoured the Internet for information about the mega soap star, checked out her Web site and viewed hours of past episodes of *P & P.* He knew that she came from a small east Texas town where she'd worked as a teenage model in a local department store before coming to Los Angeles to attend UCLA. Her first job after graduation had been as a pool secretary at Metro Artists United, a talent agency where she caught the eye of an agent who put her in a TV commercial and launched her career. She had never been married, had won two Daytime Emmys, a BET Award and an NAACP Image Award. She was devoted to her fans, whom she referred to as her family and in more than one interview she'd stated that a husband and children were most likely not in her future, as they would complicate the career goals she'd set for herself.

But is she happy? Taye wondered as he tried to throw off images of his lips easing down over hers, his hands spanning her tiny waist. Had she felt the sexual magnetism radiating between them every time they'd locked eyes? His heart turned over. Was hers doing the same? A quiver of arousal slid through him, making him shudder with startling need. God, how wonderful it would be to make love to her! But that was an impossible dream.

Jewel Blaine was smart. Professional. Driven. Secure. And certainly not easily swayed. He shouldn't have been surprised that she would question if he was the right man to direct her show.

But she'll come around, Taye told himself, sensing that he was just the man to handle a woman like her. It was going to be an incredibly exhilarating and possibly slippery experience, but he could hardly wait to get started.

* * *

It wasn't the single glass of white wine that Jewel had had with lunch that made her miscalculate the distance between her car and the utility van that suddenly stopped in front of her. She stomped on the brakes and held her breath as the mind-fog fueled by thoughts of Taye Elliott broke apart and dissolved.

"Damn!" she cursed as her front bumper connected with the spare tire riding on the back of the van—thankfully, the hunk of rubber cushioned what could have been a major impact. Jewel slumped back in her seat, angry with herself for losing control and allowing this to happen. She was a good driver with a spotless record, and the last thing she needed was a moving violation or an angry driver screaming in her face.

Through her windshield, she saw the driver of the van—a wiry Asian man in a white jumpsuit—hop out and go to the rear of his vehicle. While he inspected the damage, three more men, who looked as if they could have been the driver's brothers, emerged from the passenger side of the van and joined him. They began chattering away in a language that Jewel did not understand. However, she could certainly tell by the tone of their voices and their hand gestures that they were upset about the accident.

"Oh, hell, I gotta deal with this," Jewel muttered, flipping open the storage compartment in the dash to retrieve a card with insurance information on it. Grabbing her purse and flinging her car door open, she jumped out and looked around.

Luckily, she had turned off busy Wilshire Boulevard to take Windsor to West Eighth, and was on a side street dotted with small shops, a gas station and a huge abandoned warehouse.

"I'm so, so sorry," she began, hurrying toward the front of her car, thankful that no one was around who might recognize her and initiate a paparazzi frenzy.

"You hit me, lady!" the driver shouted, pointing to the back of his van. "You hit me hard."

"I know, I know. It was all my fault. I'll take care of any damage." Jewel offered him her insurance information, which he snatched out of her hand, glowering more hatefully at her. Jewel sucked in a deep breath, stepped over to inspect the damage and was pleasantly surprised to see that the only vehicle injured was hers—a deep scrape that ran the length of her bumper. The spare tire on the back of the van had protected the other vehicle from damage.

"Well, that's good," she said with an audible sigh of relief, using hand signals to demonstrate to the man that hers was the only vehicle with a problem. "My insurance will cover my car. No reason to call the police," she said, raising her voice. "No damage to you, thank God. No problem, right?"

The man rolled his eyes and glanced, three times, from the dent in her bumper to his unscarred van while his fellow passengers crowded around. Immediately, a rapid exchange of conversation erupted—short guttural bursts thrown back and forth, sounding very angry to Jewel, who stepped away in alarm.

Easing back toward her car, she began to worry. What were they talking about? Why were they waving their arms and screaming? Deciding that she'd better call the police after all, Jewel leaned into the open car door to get her cell phone, but when she raised her head, the driver of the van was standing in her face, screaming. He clutched his left shoulder with his right hand and bent over. "Problem, lady. Big problem. Hurt. Hurt real bad." He kept rubbing his hand back and forth over his shoulder and groaning low in his throat. His companions patted his back in sympathy making pointed frowns at Jewel.

Jewel felt her mouth go dry and the muscles in her throat clamp shut. Was this some kind of a scam? Had she been drawn into a situation that was about to turn ugly? As the realization settled in, she made a quick decision: no way was she going to fall for whatever con job or sting these men planned to pull.

Revising her approach, she turned to the driver and, using her most intimidating voice, yelled, "What in hell are you talking about?" A pause long enough for him to understand that he'd chosen the wrong sister to tangle with today. "You're hurt?" she snapped. "I did not hit you hard enough to hurt you and you sure as hell didn't have any trouble jumpin' outta your van." She almost spat the words at the man. "I hit the *spare tire*. I was going only twenty miles an hour, at most!"

"Bad. Hurt bad," the driver insisted in a more urgent groan, eyes swiveling toward his fellow passengers, who nodded their agreement.

Determined to maintain control over the situation, Jewel sniffed and then squinted suspiciously at the moaning man. "Fine. If you're really injured, I'd better call an ambulance. And the police, too." She whipped out her cell phone and held it up, almost like a gun, thumb poised, ready to launch a 911 call. Taking care to enunciate slowly and clearly, she told him, "I am calling the police. Police? Hospital? Okay?"

The driver's eyes widened in apprehension. He let go of his shoulder and waved both hands back and forth. "No. No police, lady. No hospital. You pay me cash money, okay?"

Infuriated, Jewel laughed in his face, unable to believe this brazen demand. How dare he try to shake her down? In broad daylight? She snorted in disgust and jabbed the air with her cell phone. "Pay you cash money? I don't think so. You gotta be out of your mind. I have insurance. If you're really injured, my insurance will take care of you. I'm gonna call 911 and we're gonna stay right here until the ambulance and the police arrive, then we'll see how hurt you are."

The man shouted something at his companions, who scurried back into the van. The driver spat on the pavement, hurled sharp words at Jewel and then returned to his van, taking off in a squeal of hot rubber.

Shaking with outrage, Jewel got back into her car and started the engine. Driving slowly, she paid better attention to the road and did not let her mind drift back to Taye Elliott, who'd already caused enough drama for one day.

Chapter 6

Early Saturday morning Jewel awakened feeling ravenous, so she ditched her usual wheat toast and herbal tea breakfast regime and whipped up a batch of cinnamon butter sweet rolls. The impulsive indulgence seemed perfectly logical to her, considering how much stress she was under.

Setting down her fork, Jewel crossed her arms over the silky soft fabric of her pale peach shirt, her stomach in knots and her appetite rapidly fading. Her car was wrecked. Taye was coming for dinner and she hadn't heard back from Sonny.

Why did I agree to meet with Taye tonight? she fretted. What had she been thinking, inviting him to her house? They could have met at the studio, or in a private room in a restaurant, or at Fred Warner's business office in downtown L.A. Anyplace less intimate than her home.

Jewel shoved aside her icing-laced sweet roll when the telephone rang. She snatched it up and scowled into the receiver as Sonny told her he could not make it to her meeting with Taye tonight. Family commitment. He'd catch up with her Monday.

Frustrated, Jewel jabbed the button to end the call and focused on the back door as it suddenly opened.

The woman who entered the kitchen was humming, an iPod device plugged into her ears.

"Hello, Carmie," Jewel called over to her assistant, who removed her ear plugs, made three quick turns to wrap the black wires around her music player and then acknowledged Jewel with a short half wave as she pocketed her keys and shut the door.

Carmie Lewis was the woman who took care of both the mundane and the extravagant details that made up Jewel Blaine's life. She was Jewel's go-to person, secretary, trusted friend and her conscience, too, when the situation required.

Carmie was petite, almost as short as Jewel, but heavier in the hips and thighs. She had butter-cream skin, textured copper-red hair that dangled in tight curls around a wise face, cheek-bones that any professional model would kill for and wide-set brown eyes that drew attention away from the sprinkling of freckles that marched across the bridge of her upturned nose. At forty-three, she was as hip, sassy and attractive as a woman ten years younger.

"Thanks for coming over so fast," Jewel added, sounding a tad apologetic, knowing how bad traffic on the 405 could be between Ladera Heights and her home in Brentwood. Monday through Friday, Carmie managed Jewel's correspondence, kept her calendars on track, organized her wardrobe to ensure that Jewel's clothing delivered a diva punch without looking slutty, did the grocery shopping and most of the cooking. In fact, Carmie was an excellent cook who enjoyed showing off her skill, with special meals for her busy, on-the-go employer.

"Sure you didn't have plans this morning?" Jewel asked.

"Nope. Just like I said, coming over now is fine, but I've gotta leave here by two. Hair appointment that I can't afford to miss." Carmie removed her reflective sunglasses and stuck them into the side pocket of her purse. "I stopped by Royal Street Market and picked up a pint of mango sherbet for dessert." She plunked her leather patchwork purse down on the gold-flecked granite counter separating the kitchen from the breakfast area and then stuck the sherbet in the freezer. "So, what do you want for dinner?" Carmie asked as she went to the sink and washed her hands.

"Something simple, light and in the fridge…ready for me to heat up and serve."

"No problem." Carmie paused, frowning. "And what's that you're eating?" she asked, wrinkling her nose at Jewel's plate.

"Cinnamon sweet rolls."

"Uh-oh. What's wrong? Only time you make those things is when something or someone's gotten to you."

With a flick of her wrist, Jewel dismissed her assistant's comment. "Nothing's wrong. In fact, things couldn't be better. Guess I wasn't as hungry as I thought," Jewel feigned, pushing her plate aside.

"Well, I'm not surprised you're stressin' out and eatin' all that sugar," Carmie stated with the authority that came from three years of working for the actress, "with all that's been going on. First, Brad up and dies, then you get a stunt director in charge of your show and next, some Koreans try to shake you down on your way home. I told you, you need a driver. Why you insist on driving yourself around L.A. I don't understand. Los Angeles can be a dangerous place for a woman out and about alone. You need to be more careful. If *I* could afford it, I'd keep a chauffeured car on call 24/7 'cause driving is one thing I could easily give up."

"First of all, I didn't say they were Koreans. Asians. That's all I said," Jewel clarified, having anticipating Carmie's reaction to what happened.

"Okay, Asians," Carmie conceded. "Doesn't matter who they are, they oughta be arrested for trying a stunt like that."

Jewel ignored the remark and went on. "And second, I don't mind the driving. Being alone in the car with my music is kinda nice. Makes me feel safe, not insecure or helpless. As if I can really take care of myself."

"Is it the freedom you like or the control?"

Carmie's question was dead serious, giving Jewel pause. As a television actress, she was surrounded by people assigned to take care of her makeup, her hair, her body, her schedule and even the meals she ate. It seemed as if some eager man or woman was always standing nearby, prepared to do things for Jewel that she had once enjoyed doing for herself. Driving her own car to work every day was her last hold on an independence she was reluctant to give up. However, she had to agree with her assistant. "All right. I want both freedom and control! So what? And please don't play Doctor Phil with me today, okay?"

With a louder-than-usual huff, Carmie bobbed her head up and down. "All right. Don't want my advice? I'll shut up." She went back to getting her meal together, while commenting over her shoulder. "My son has all of those *Terror Train* DVDs and I've watched 'em with him and his friends a few times. They're absolutely wild! The body count is so high you can't keep up with who's killin' who. And the sex? Whew! It's a whole lot raunchier than anything you've ever done on *P & P.* Closer to soft porn, I'd say. You think Taye Elliott's gonna spice things up in the bedroom between Caprice and Darin? Let 'em get down and dirty? Do some serious lovin', you know?"

Jewel made a noncommittal sound in the back of her throat. *Spice things up? Get down and dirty? Hell, no!* Caprice was sensuous, seductive and sexy. Nothing remotely close to soft porn was going to appear on a network show. Surely, Taye Elliott knew how far he could push the censors, didn't he? If not, she'd make sure to discuss that with Taye tonight.

"Have you seen any of his movies?" Carmie inquired, opening the refrigerator to remove a bag of grated cheese.

"No, of course not." *Action flicks are not my thing.*

"Well, why don't you rent one, watch it before he shows up tonight?"

"Think I should?" *Why? So we can talk car chases and rollovers all evening? Or analyze fake orgasms and equally fake tits?*

"Absolutely!" Carmie was emphatic.

"Well, I'll think about it," Jewel vaguely responded, wondering if Carmie might have a point. Perhaps viewing Mr. Elliott's work would give her a better feel for his creative approach as well as ammunition for any disagreements they might have over his vision for *P & P.* "Are they in stock at Movieland?"

"Oh, I'm sure they'd have all of 'em," Carmie replied. "But you'd better get over there before noon. After that, all the good movies are gone."

"Hmm, maybe I'll do that," Jewel decided, leaving the kitchen and heading toward her bedroom.

Passing through the den, she paused at the bay window overlooking the shimmering aqua pool that swept the curve of the flagstone patio. Her favorite pink rosebush was in flower, creating a vibrant splash of color against the lush green foliage in the yard. She smiled, recalling that Brad Fortune had given her that rosebush as a housewarming gift when she first moved in. She loved her house in Brentwood. It was small enough to manage on her own, yet large enough to entertain a crowd of friends when she felt like throwing a party. The one-story Mediterranean white stucco house was the perfect home for her, where she, Brad and Sonny had spent quite a few Saturday afternoons by the pool, running lines and drinking margaritas while strategizing Caprice and Darin's next moves. Jewel shuddered, throwing off the memories, unable to imagine doing the same with Taye Elliott.

Leaving the den, Jewel went into her bedroom to retrieve her purse and her car keys. Hurrying through the kitchen, she called out to Carmie, "Be right back!" While waiting for the garage door to rise, she tried to calculate how many *Terror Train* films she could watch before Taye showed up at six o'clock.

Chapter 7

When the phone rang, Taye clicked Pause on the remote control and stilled the image of Caprice Desmond kissing Darin Saintclare in the backseat of a dark limousine. The episode of *The Proud and the Passionate* that he'd been watching was the last of Brad Fortune's work and from it, Taye had been able to detect nuances in the characters that he wanted to recapture when he took over as director.

Now, he checked the caller ID on the phone, saw the name "Elliott," paused, took a deep breath and then reached for the handset.

"Hey, Cliff," he said, greeting his younger brother, the only member of his family to whom he spoke on a regular basis.

"Taye. Just checkin' in. Hadn't heard from you for a while, man," Cliff replied in an upbeat tone. "Been thinking about you… What's up out there in la-la land?"

"Nothing much," Taye hedged, not ready to tell his brother the truth: a hell of a lot was going on. He had a new gig at CBC. He was entering the world of daytime drama. He was totally smitten with a soap star named Jewel Blaine and thought he was falling in love. But now was not the time to elaborate on his chaotic show-business lifestyle, which was much more exotic and unstable than his brother's predictable world.

Cliff was a steady, reliable lawyer with a wife, two daughters and a home in the suburbs of Pittsburgh. His life was safe, orderly and totally removed from the shifting, gutsy environment in which Taye moved, where everything could change in a heartbeat. A deal could be canceled with a phone call. A contract broken via e-mail. A director could be fired and replaced within the span of a day, without ever being told why he was no longer needed. In Taye's line of work, nothing was certain until it was over—until the film was on the screen, the principals had been paid and the royalties started rolling in. Until that happened, it was all speculation and he'd learned to live with the insecurities of his chosen career.

"I saw the latest *Terror Train.* Good stuff, man," Cliff said. "I took Sandra to one of those advance screenings in the mall. She really got into the movie and she's not one for action flicks, you know? The love story was what she liked best. But that gas station explosion? That was the bomb, man. Too wild!"

"Glad you guys enjoyed it," Taye replied, then there was silence for a moment. Cliff, his wife, Sandra, and their two daughters had visited Taye in Los Angeles last year, ending a family estrangement that began when Taye defied his father and left Pittsburgh to launch his acting career. All year, Cliff had been trying to bring their tiny family back together and Taye was beginning to feel guilty for not doing more to make that happen.

"So, what're you workin' on now? Another movie?" Cliff asked.

"No. Not now. I'm doing TV. A great opportunity that's gonna be a lot of fun," Taye hedged, hesitant to go into details. After all, the directing job was only for a soap opera, not a made-for-TV movie with A-list stars. A temporary fill-in until the end of the sweeps. But why did he feel so uneasy talking

about it? Did he worry that his work was somehow less important than his brother's, his father's? Why did he feel like he had
to prove himself repeatedly? He was making a damn good
living and had no reason to feel ashamed. He was as successful as his brothers, wasn't he?

"Yeah? Television? Any show I might watch?" Cliff wanted
to know.

"No, probably not," Taye responded. "I start Monday.… I'll
fill you in later, once I get a feel for how it's gonna play out."
Eager to move on, Taye changed the subject, inquiring after his
father and other two brothers, whom he had not seen in years.

As Cliff filled Taye in on the family happenings, Taye's
mind slipped back to the day he decided to drop out of medical
school, leave Pittsburgh and head to Los Angeles to try his luck
in the movies. His decision had infuriated and disappointed his
father, Dr. Roland Elliott, the respected reconstructive surgeon
who had invested hundreds of thousands of dollars in each of
his sons' educations with the expectation that they join the
family business—The Elliott Cosmetic Surgery Center.

Taye's three brothers went along with their father's plan and
earned degrees in medicine. Don specialized in nose jobs, eyes
and face-lifts. William preferred liposuction and breast aug-
mentation. And Cliff, who went back to law school to become
a medical attorney, skillfully handled the legal challenges from
clients who'd expected miracle results.

When Taye tossed away his chance at a career in medicine,
brothers Don and William had blasted him for being foolish and
naive, calling him ungrateful and selfish for allowing their
father to fund his education when he had never intended to
complete medical school. Only Cliff had sided with Taye, sup-
porting his decision to go his own way.

Over the years, Taye had tried to repay his father's invest-
ment, but his checks always came back, uncashed. This
refusal deeply hurt Taye, who saw it as a blatant rejection of
all he had accomplished, further hardening his heart toward
his father. He spoke to his dad on Father's Day and Christ-

mas Day, in conversations that were one-sided and brief. Taye missed the close relationship he'd once enjoyed with his family, but wasn't sorry about the career choice he'd made.

"We need to get together. All of us," Cliff was pressing. "Dad's getting older, the kids are growing up and time is passin', bro. Think about coming home for a visit this summer, okay?"

"Yeah, sure. I'll think about it," Taye agreed, knowing that would never happen. He had too much to take care of in L.A.

After hanging up, Taye put Cliff's call out of his mind and resumed the DVD he'd been watching. In less than half an hour, he had to be at Jewel's house, but he wanted to see how the episode concluded.

Watching closely, Taye studied Caprice Desmond as she snaked her arms around Darin Saintclare's neck and smothered him with a kiss. It was long and deep, ending when she slid her hands down to rest them on Darin's thighs, very near his crotch. The scene brought a surge of heat into Taye's belly, initiating an unexpected hard-on.

But I'm a hell of a lucky guy, Taye decided. He was actually going to direct that gorgeous woman! Watch her every move through the camera lens. Listen to her sexy voice, inhale her perfume and spend hours in conversations that he hoped would spill off the set and into more intimate settings. Taye shook his head, knowing he shouldn't have such cozy thoughts about an actress under his direction, but couldn't help himself. Engaging in a fantasy romantic encounter with Jewel Blaine was the only indulgence he could afford.

I wonder what she's doing right now? He let his thoughts wander. *Getting ready for our meeting? Stepping out of the shower?* He could just imagine what she looked like wrapped in nothing but a towel, a damp swell of soft tan breasts peeking over the fold of white terry cloth.

Blinking away that vision, he refocused on the television where the romantic scene in the limo was giving way to a lover's quarrel about Caprice and Darin's upcoming separation.

Taye kept one eye on the flat-screen TV as their argument unfolded and continued to dress, stepping into a pair of navy slacks and pulling on a crisp white shirt.

When the credits began to roll, Taye paused to think over what he'd just seen, realizing he'd expected much more emotion from Caprice at the end. More desperation. Remorse. Even fear. In Taye's opinion, the scene had not inflicted enough emotional damage to the couple's rocky relationship. It had been a predictable, satisfying exchange, but Taye would have done it differently.

Taye wanted Caprice Desmond to show more spunk, deliver more spark. As it stood, Caprice was coming off as a tiger that had been tamed. A domesticated wildcat seething with desire, which needed to break free.

Taye tapped his key chain against his thigh and mulled the episode, knowing Caprice's undercurrent of simmering emotion had teased him, lured him into anticipating a climactic explosion that simply hadn't materialized. He felt cheated and let down.

It's time for Caprice Desmond to create some havoc, he decided. *Become a mega diva wildcat that the fans will absolutely love…or hate. Either way, they'll watch every episode to see what she's gonna do.*

Taye knew how to get what he wanted on film. He'd moved audiences, literally, to the edges of their seats, infusing them with awe, shock and fear laced with hope. He could do the same for the fans of *P & P* by making them hunger for Caprice Desmond's next move like chocolate junkies craving a fix. He planned to engage and outrage her fans, encouraging them to cry for more. What Jewel Blaine needed was a director who could expose and exploit the raw undercurrent of heat that Taye knew she possessed. *And I'm the one to do it,* he vowed, knowing it could happen now that he was in control.

Chapter 8

The loose yellow-and-tan-print cardigan, paired with sleek chocolate-brown leggings, was the perfect backdrop for the chunky tiger's eye and butterscotch jade necklace that Jewel bought last summer in Hong Kong. Two tortoiseshell cuff bracelets stacked on one arm and ballerina flats in metallic tones of gold and rust completed her casual at-home outfit. A short blast of Glossy Girl hair shine over the curls she'd arranged in a bouncy cascade at the back of her head and Jewel was ready for her meeting with Taye.

Deciding what to wear tonight had taken up the better part of the afternoon as Jewel pawed her way through her massive walk-in closet, examining different outfits. At work, her character's clothes were like props, extensions of Caprice Desmond's personality and attitude that helped set a mood or define her motivation. Caprice was a clotheshorse diva with an extensive *P & P* wardrobe that was trendy, hip and fashion-setting edgy. However, when Jewel Blaine was out of camera range and ready to relax at home, she preferred comfortable, easy-to-wear pieces that reflected her more conservative side.

The doorbell rang at exactly six o'clock. As Jewel had expected, Taye was on time and when he shook hands with her, in what she thought was a much-too-formal manner, her anxiety level dropped and the tension she'd been carrying around all day vanished.

What had she been worried about? she wondered, knowing she'd allowed her mind to conjure up wild scenarios about his arrival: that he would lean in and make an air-kiss just below her ear. That he would give her a firm hug of welcome, bringing his body in touch with hers. That he would make some flip remark that would shift their meeting from a discussion about *P & P* into a more personal zone. Clearly, she'd worried for no reason.

"Hi. Glad you could make it," she told Taye, letting go of his hand and waving him through the candle-lit foyer toward the den. She was struck once again by his fresh lemony scent and wondered if it came from the soap he used or his cologne. Either way, she knew she liked it very much.

"Hey, I'm just glad you were able to squeeze me in. Hope meeting here at your house hasn't inconvenienced you," Taye remarked in a breezy manner.

Jewel laughed as she escorted Taye over to the white leather sectional that faced open French doors leading onto the patio. The first streaks of an orange-red sunset shimmered in the pool's dark water.

"Great pool," Taye remarked, walking over to the door to look out into the yard. "You a good swimmer?"

When he turned to look back at her, Jewel opened her mouth, thought a minute and then ducked her head in embarrassment. "I have to confess…I'm not. But I do water aerobics in the pool with my trainer a few times a month. I play around in the shallow end, swim a few laps now and then, but I don't dive off the board into the deep end. That's where I draw the line."

Taye stuck a hand into the pocket of his navy slacks and tilted his head to one side, an inquisitive expression overtaking his features. "Really? I'm surprised you don't swim. Why not?"

"I dunno. I think my fear of diving started when I took swimming lessons back home in Texas. It was not a good experience."

"Too bad, but you do look like the swimming type," Taye observed.

"Oh? And what's that?"

"Clearly you're in great shape and you don't strike me as the type who goes in for lifting weights in the gym."

"You're right. I don't."

"Tennis, then, perhaps?" he probed.

A hint of a smile teased the corners of her mouth as Jewel shook her head. "Not at all."

"Power walking, the treadmill?"

"You got me. That's what I like to do."

"Hmm, hmm. I thought so. You like to be toned, but not bulky. You like cardio, but prefer to do it alone. I'd guess you're not much into competitive sports. Am I right?"

"You're very observant," Jewel commented, actually appreciative of his remarks. "Do you always pay such close attention to the exercise regimes of your actors?"

"I'm a director, remember? I watch actors all day. Size them up. Figure out what works for them."

When he scanned her with a slow shift of his eyes, Jewel escaped his pointed assessment by moving behind the bar on the other side of the room. "What can I get you to drink?" Jewel asked.

"What do you suggest?" Taye responded, still standing by the door, resting one shoulder on the frame, watching her with measured eyes.

Jewel raised a bottle with a colorful sunburst label on the front. "I can recommend this crisp chardonnay from the vineyard of a friend of mine who lives in the Russian River Valley."

"Sounds perfect. Want me to open it?"

"No, that's okay. I've got it," she said, feeling his gaze on her hands as she worked the opener into the cork and poured the wine into two marquis cut crystal glasses. She was thankful that the marble-topped bar provided a barrier between them and support for her to steady herself.

"Tell me more about your nonswimming life," he continued in a playful tone. "You blame it on what again?" Taye approached, accepted the glass of wine and took a sip. "Very nice," he murmured with a satisfied nod as he settled on a bar stool across from her.

Jewel leaned over, both arms on the bar, chin up, thinking back. "I waited too late to start taking lessons," she decided, picking up their conversation. "I was thirteen years old. Didn't want to get my hair wet, didn't want the boys in my class to see me in a swimsuit and didn't want water up my nose. I did everything possible to stay out of the pool."

"That's too bad. Ever think about taking lessons again?"

"Absolutely not. I'm happy to sit by my pool and drink in the sun and watch others splash around."

"You prefer to play it safe, huh?"

"Sometimes," she tossed back. "Depends on what's going on."

"You never know when you'll find yourself in a dangerous situation. Where you'll have to take a chance."

"But that doesn't happen very often," Jewel tossed back.

A long beat while they locked eyes.

Jewel walked from behind the bar. "I'm rarely blindsided by something that I know I can avoid," she remarked, successfully disarming his banter. "Why don't we eat before getting down to business?" she suggested, motioning for Taye to follow her into the dining room where they helped themselves to the seafood quesadillas and jicama salad that Carmie had prepared.

Moving to the round glass-topped table near the patio door, they ate, drank wine and chatted about industry-related topics like the blockbuster opening of the latest *Batman* movie and how action films were raking in big bucks. This was the perfect opening for Jewel to tell Taye, "I enjoyed *Terror Train 1, 2* and *3* very much."

He almost choked on a mouthful of salad. "You saw them?" he blurted, seeming genuinely surprised.

Jewel let a slow, secret grin ease over her face, enjoying the shocked expression that overtook Taye's features and glad she'd taken Carmie's advice. "Yes, I rented them this morning and watched all afternoon, although I have to admit that I squeezed them in between phone calls back and forth with my insurance company and the Lexus car dealership."

"Oh? Something wrong with your car?"

"Nothing serious. I had a minor fender bender on the way home yesterday."

"After lunch?"

"Yea. My fault. Not paying attention. Guess I was distracted."

"By what?"

"Nothing important," she lied.

"Were you hurt?"

"No. No one was injured."

"That's good."

"Right. So, I'll take my car in to be fixed Monday. Insurance will cover it and that's all there is to that." She shrugged. "One of those stupid self-inflicted scratches."

A knowing grin. "Happens to all of us sooner or later. Need a ride to the studio Monday?"

"No, the dealer will have a driver take me in and, hopefully, deliver my car back to me by the time I'm ready to leave."

"Good. Now…about my movies…you really enjoyed them? Truthfully?"

"Yes, I did, but in the second film, how did you convince Marilu Gale to squeeze into that child-size bed with Danny Lowe for their love scene? It was so cramped in that sleeping car! Must have been a claustrophobic situation for everyone involved."

Taye laughed, agreeing. "It was. As I remember, there was nothing romantic about that scene. Blazing one-hundred-degree heat in the desert, trapped inside a stripped-down train for nine hours, with too many people and too many complaints. Whew! That was not a memorable shoot."

"If the public only knew what you directors put your actors through…" Jewel teased, letting her sentence drift off as she got up and went back to the buffet table. "Ready for dessert? Then we get to work, okay? You've gotta taste Carmie's lemon cream pie."

"Sounds perfect," Taye agreed, accepting a generous slice of the creamy confection Jewel handed to him.

When they had finished eating, they spread their scripts and yellow legal pads out between them, as if afraid to allow an unscripted moment to slip in and challenge their all-about-work agenda.

Tipping his head slightly toward Jewel, Taye launched into his assessment of the status of *P & P* and then listened to what she had to say, making it clear that he was extremely interested in her opinion.

"I think Darin has the bigger problem and that he's trying to make it look as if Caprice is at fault," Taye remarked after Jewel's recap of the latest plotline. "He's ruthless, power-hungry, scheming. And he has Caprice fooled into thinking she won't be affected by his problems. What might work is to change Caprice's direction." Taye paused, sipping from his wineglass. He was about to go on when Jewel interrupted.

"Where do you think Caprice ought to be?" she queried, wanting to hear what Taye had in mind.

"Into her messiest confrontation yet. Where Caprice will have to carry the weight…you know, become the heavy and let Darin get more sympathy. I viewed the footage of the scene in the limo…where Darin pushes Caprice to come home. She's gotta be desperate enough to make Darin fear their relationship might implode. I want her to inflict more emotional damage. Their romance is too predictable, satisfying but not electrifying. She's gotta absolutely refuse to go along with Darin, sending him into total confusion."

Jewel sat forward, making a small jerk of surprise with her shoulders. Something in Taye's remark had alarmed her. "I don't know about that, Taye. That's not the way Brad wanted the scene to play."

"Brad's no longer the director."

His words were clear and firm. So terse they sent a flash of annoyance through Jewel, who promptly replied, "But you told Fred and me that you planned to stick close to Brad's interpretation, even use some of his footage as flashbacks."

"Yes, I did." Taye hunched over the table, a somber mood emerging. "But I've changed my mind. I want to reshoot the limo scene and maybe the beach scene, too."

"Go back on location in Texas?" Jewel groaned. Hitting the road again was not high on her agenda. Too much turmoil, drama and friction. All she wanted to do was to stay home and get back to her normal routine.

"Not far. I can shoot closer to home, on Catalina Island. No need to go back to Galveston. But it's gotta be reshot because it's not on the mark."

"In what way?" Jewel prodded, beginning to wonder if Taye Elliott was a man whose word meant very little. "What's on your mind, Taye?"

"Flipping Caprice's reaction to Darin completely."

"You want to change Caprice's motivation?" Jewel gave him a disbelieving chuckle. "Why?"

"So she can push back harder. State what she wants in a way that shows how desperate *she* is. After all, she's got a lot to lose, too. I just don't like that undertone of weakness that I'm getting. Regret weakens any character."

Jewel didn't respond right away, but simply sat quietly and listened as Taye forged ahead with his vision in an overconfident rush to prove what he could do. When he'd finished talking, she spoke up.

"Sorry, Taye. I totally disagree. Making Caprice so overtly aggressive will be disastrous. She's aware of the damage she's done. She's gotta be contrite and vulnerable…this keeps the tension high."

"No…it doesn't," Taye rejected with a snap. "It keeps

Caprice in check when she needs to cut loose and challenge her self-imposed inhibitions."

"But she's not the real risk-taker. Darin is. There's a predictable sense of stability and cautiousness that fans expect of Caprice. Altering that would destroy a major character trait that I've worked hard to develop. Caprice Desmond is a unique person. Complicated, yet easily accepted…*if* you understand her extensive backstory." *Which, obviously, you don't,* Jewel was tempted to add. Sitting back, she crossed her arms at her waist and waited for Taye's reply.

The whir of the pool sweeper making its way across the water filled an awkward pause. When Taye broke into a wide grin of defeat, she flinched. "Touché," he conceded, jabbing the air with his index finger, giving Jewel her props. "You know your character better than I ever could, so we'll keep her reaction as you played it, but I still plan to reshoot the beach scene on Catalina so our visuals will be consistent now that we're staying in California."

"Sounds fine," Jewel stated, pleased that they'd been able to compromise so easily, and certain Lori Callyer, *P & P*'s head writer, would certainly back Jewel up. "I appreciate your taking my input into consideration. Brad, Lori and I could usually work through these kinds of glitches and compromise." She sighed in relief. "You know what, Taye? This get-together was a good idea. We're on such a cramped shooting schedule and we've got so much work to do, this will help us move more quickly Monday."

"I hear you," Taye agreed.

"Thanks for agreeing not to change Caprice…or me." Her voice slipped low, her words fading into a hush.

Taye slowly lifted his palm toward Jewel and rocked her with a steady gaze. "Don't worry, Jewel. Changing *anything* about you is the furthest thing from my mind. I like you just the way you are."

Jewel felt her entire body go on alert as his remark resonated through her veins. His intent was so obvious. She gave him a slow blink of her eyes, knowing if she tried to talk, she might blunder into territory that ought to be avoided. After composing herself, she spoke her mind. "Taye, we can either dance around this issue all night or clear the air right now."

"I'm listening," Taye replied, cool and unruffled.

His wide-eyed, little-boy innocent expression rattled Jewel's nerves. She inhaled a stream of air and then swallowed with a gulp. "Taye, I *will* follow your direction and give you my best performance. Every day. Every take. We'll work closely together, perhaps become friends. But that's all. I want you to understand that I'm all about business. The success of *P & P* is all I care about, okay? There can't be any reason for either of us to feel uneasy working together. Got that?"

When he didn't reply, Jewel rose from her chair, went to stand behind it and leaned against its back. Studying Taye as she steadied herself, she waited for his reply, hating that his crooked half smile was turning her insides into jelly. "Agreed?" she pressed again.

His nod implied an affirmative answer, but the expression on his face sent Jewel a completely different signal.

Taye wished desperately that she was not Jewel Blaine, the actress he'd have to face on the set every day, because at that moment all he wanted to do was corner her behind that bar and push her up against that cool black granite, press his tongue between those full red lips, nibble her earlobe and ease himself deep into what he imagined was a sizzling-hot center that needed cooling down. But that wasn't going to happen, so he'd better get a grip and pull himself together. With a jerk of his chin, Taye forced the blood zinging through his veins to calm down, told his heart to stop thumping so raggedly in his chest, unstuck his tongue from the roof of his mouth and ran it over his lower lip.

He checked his watch. Time to leave. Two hours was all she had promised to give him and he didn't want to overstay his welcome. Standing, he began to gather his scripts and notepads filled with the results of their meeting. He slipped the documents into his briefcase while reminding himself that this temporary shot at daytime directing was his best chance to prove what he could do in a medium that was exploding. Satellite, cable and on-demand material downloaded straight from the Internet onto a television screen made for great potential. This new medium could become the cash cow to secure his financial future and he had no intention of blowing this job.

From the corner of his eye Taye could see Jewel approaching and could tell by the click of her heels on the terrazzo tile floor that she was moving rather quickly. He looked up, caught her standing close at his side, scrutinizing him as if she wanted to ask a question—as if his silence was confusing.

"You're absolutely right," he quickly concurred before she could make another comment. "I'll never give you a reason for either of us to feel uneasy on the set. That's a promise." His words had popped out of his mouth without any real thought and he wasn't exactly sure he'd wanted to agree with her. Whatever was pulling him so strongly to this woman had gotten a hold on her, too. He'd felt it when she first shook his hand, seen it in her face when she'd opened the door tonight and knew it was going to remain at the edges of their relationship as they worked together on *P & P*.

Rattled by the tumble of thoughts that were crashing into one another, Taye stilled his body and said, "Now that that is straightened out, let's get on with making this season the best one ever." Then he winked at Jewel, one slow, lazy blink that sent a zap of fire through her, hoping to bring out the humor in the situation.

Jewel broke into laughter and made a joking retort that he didn't hear because he was so busy processing the startling effect this woman had on him. *Thank God she has a sense of humor! She isn't really mad at me and not as cool and uptight as she's trying to make me believe.*

"Until Monday, then," he told her, his features softening with a slow smile. Briefcase in hand, he moved toward the entry while telling himself, *The only way I can gain Jewel Blaine's respect and trust is to devote myself totally to getting along with her while putting my talent on display. I've gotta show her and the studio execs that I'm the perfect man for the job.*

"Sure. See you Monday. At ten, right?" Jewel stated, breaking into Taye's silent, fast-paced plotting.

"Oh, yeah. Sure," he answered, clearly distracted by his own internal banter.

In a formal farewell gesture, he offered Jewel his right hand. She took it, squeezed it hard and then fixed him with a look that told him she was grateful that the evening was ending on a friendly, positive note. Glancing over her head, Taye mischievously raised two fingers of his left hand. "No drastic changes in Caprice's character. Scout's honor."

Her face beamed satisfaction and relief, a clear indication that he was earning her trust. She opened her front door

"And thanks for dinner, too," he added. "I'm glad we were able to talk."

"Me, too, but it's really time for you to go," she added, waving him toward the open door.

"I know, I know," Taye replied, but for some reason he could not move. She sounded calm, but not totally in control of her voice. Was this the moment he'd been waiting for? The right time to say what had been on his mind? "You know, Jewel, I'm thrilled to have the opportunity to direct you, but at the same time, I wish we weren't working together."

"Oh? I'm surprised. And what would happen if we weren't working together?" she teased right back, watching for his reaction.

"Sure you really want to know?"

"Of course."

"This," he whispered, pressing his index finger first to his lips and then placing it gently to hers.

Neither Taye nor Jewel moved a muscle as they remained connected for an electrified moment.

"Is that all you have to offer?" she huskily challenged, shifting gently away from his touch.

Taye's confidence gathered strength. She wasn't as upset as he'd feared she might be and he'd definitely stirred a reaction. "For now, yes," he said, not about to push his luck. Turning away, he walked out the door and across the brick-paved driveway, holding his breath while very much aware that Jewel was still standing there, watching him.

Chapter 9

The Call to the Altar at Mount Olive Friendship Church was Marlena Kirk's favorite part of the lively Sunday service, which included song, praise, testimony and long-winded sermons that left the congregation exhausted but spiritually inspired.

As a soulful rendition of "Take My Hand, Precious Lord" surged from the lofty pipe organ, Marlena slipped out of her pew and stood. Tall, with ebony skin, striking sharp-planed features and a flair for wearing colorful Afrocentric dress, she walked up the center aisle, sank to her knees at the sturdy wooden railing surrounding the pulpit, bent her head and clasped her hands together in prayer.

First, she worked her way through her usual prayer requests for the health, spiritual growth and wealth of family, close friends and fellow church members. Next, she started on her extensive list of clients, those who depended on her to keep them not only gainfully employed, but also happily employed and in demand.

As a successful agent to some of Hollywood's most visible

and steady-working actors, comedians, musicians, dancers and writers, Marlena believed that including her clients in her Sunday-morning prayer ritual enhanced their creative talents, kept them physically and emotionally healthy and improved her odds of having a financially rewarding week.

After praying for stand-up funny man Jammy James to emerge from drug rehab with his quirky talent intact and for teen idol Delores De Love's surprise pregnancy to stay a secret for as long as possible, Marlena focused on Jewel Blaine. It didn't seem like Jewel required heavy prayer-lifting today, but she was certainly teetering on the cusp.

Marlena Kirk met Jewel Blaine when they were students at UCLA, both with dreams of careers in Hollywood. During those lean days, they'd shared a one-room studio apartment near the campus, a skimpy wardrobe of jeans and shirts and a red convertible Volkswagen car with nearly bald tires and no radio.

After graduation, Jewel focused on her goal of becoming a television actress, while Marlena launched a talent agency from the kitchen table of their apartment. When Jewel was offered her first television commercial—for a sanitizing hand cleaner that smelled like gardenias—Marlena negotiated the contract. Since then, she'd stuck with Jewel through the ensuing ups and downs of her career, faithfully representing her friend until she managed to get Jewel an audition for the role of Caprice Desmond on the groundbreaking black soap *The Proud and the Passionate*. With that coup under her belt, Marlena quickly became a sought-after agent with more clients than she could handle.

Marlena was proud to claim Jewel Blaine as her best friend as well as a professional partner—a rarity in the dog-eat-dog, me-first world of entertainment. Marlena had a reputation as a go-for-the-gold agent who worked hard for her clients, spoke the truth and was always on the prowl for the next big deal. Her strong personality, and even stronger desire to protect her clients' interests, often led to long, involved negotiations, but she was a shrewd decision maker who operated on gut impulse while considering every possible option.

Now, lips moving, but not making a sound, Marlena offered up a prayer over Jewel's situation. *The Proud and the Passionate* was beginning to slip in the ratings, while the newest daytime drama, *Down for Love,* was on the rise.

This past Friday, Marlena had taken a meeting with the producer of *DFL,* who was hot to get Jewel Blaine on his team. However, Marlena wasn't convinced that her client should make this move, but she'd promised to get back to him after conferring with Jewel…and God.

Jewel had three more years on her contract with *P & P.* CBC was counting on her to bolster the ratings and win May sweeps. Jewel was not an actress who would walk away from a challenge or disregard a commitment. A new director was just starting at *P & P,* but could he regain lost ground and bring home a winner?

This swirl of questions descended on Marlena, making her slightly dizzy. Should she encourage Jewel to jump ship before the downward spiral at *P & P* gained such momentum that the show flatlined? Would Jewel, who was such a control freak when it came to honoring obligations and following her career-guiding rules, be open to breaking her contract to go over to the competition? Or should she advise Jewel to ride it out and hope that Taye Elliott, who knew nothing about daytime TV, would turn the tide and bring the show around?

So many options. Such a dilemma. Definite challenges that Marlena faced. And as the organ music swelled to a crescendo, Marlena kept on praying.

Chapter 10

Jewel spent most Sundays reading newspapers, catching up on personal e-mails, autographing stacks of glossy photographs and memorizing lines for the upcoming week, unless Marlena coached her out for Sunday services at her church. *Right now, Marlena is probably down on her knees praying for her next contract,* Jewel mused, folding up the *L.A. Times* and putting the bulky newspaper into the recycle basket in her home office. Next, she reached for one of the eight-by-ten glossies destined for either a fan club president, a relative of an industry colleague or for use at a charity event or studio promotion.

Jewel took care to add a special remark, a note of thanks or a word of encouragement when she signed her name, knowing the recipients were the lifelines to the pulse of the public. A personalized photo was a small way of thanking those who supported her, to let them know that she gave every performance for their satisfaction.

Jewel never took her fans for granted. They were her family—they cared about her, worried with her, celebrated with her and often referred to Jewel as the black Susan Lucci: an actress with staying power, dramatic beauty, grit and graciousness. The flood of cards, teddy bears, flowers and small gifts that regularly arrived at the studio both astounded and pleased Jewel, fueling her devotion to her dedicated audience. With legions of loyal fans in the powerhouse world of daytime drama, Jewel was committed to protecting her hard-won reputation and delivering performances that excited her adoring public.

Uncapping her pen, Jewel signed her name in a diagonal splash across the bottom of one photo, then another, while her thoughts swung back to the night before. The meeting with Taye had gone well and she was relieved that he'd agreed to keep Caprice's reaction to Darin as she'd played it under Brad's direction. Maybe working with him wasn't going to be as difficult as she'd thought.

Jewel touched her lips, recalling the crazy finger-kiss he'd planted there. Why hadn't she slapped his face? Let him know how out of line he'd been? Told him not to assume she would accept such behavior?

Because you enjoyed it, stupid, she told herself, unable to keep from admiring his bold move, unable to deny that his unexpected digit-smooch had left her yearning for the real thing. But that could not happen. Starting Monday, she'd make sure Taye understood that she would be his artistic colleague, his coworker, his friend. Nothing more.

Half an hour later, Jewel slipped the final autographed photo back into the folder, ready for Carmie to put into envelopes and mail. Powering up her laptop, she worked through the numerous e-mails that had accumulated in the past two days and then impulsively decided to do a search on Taye Elliott just to see what might pop up.

"Wow," she whispered, amazed by the extensive list of Web sites containing references to Taye. She clicked on several, which mostly dealt with the *Terror Train* series, and then entered a site entitled Behind the Scenes.

Under the heading Stunt Actors, she searched his name. A quarter-page photo of Taye emerged, accompanied by an article about the accident in which he'd injured his back. *Stunt double Taye Elliott was seriously injured in a rollover car crash while doubling for Mario Van Peebles in* Hit 'Em Hard. *His career in action films may be over...*

Jewel raced through the details of his accident, recovery and eventual move into directing. Impressed with how much he'd accomplished in such a short time, she scrutinized his photo more closely. It had been taken in an outdoor setting, where rugged mountains rose in the background and horses roamed an open plain. Taye was squinting beyond the camera, as if looking off into the distance, deep in thought. He was bare-chested—rippling abs, bulging biceps and smooth chest muscles on full display, wearing well-worn jeans that rested low enough on his hips to expose a feathering of abdomen hair just above the buckle of his wide silver belt.

A warm curl of pressure settled sweetly between Jewel's legs, making her press her thighs together and scoot back in her chair, lips parted in frustration and awe.

The macho pose sent a clear and dangerous message: Taye Elliott was a guy who loved wild terrain, was ready for action and could play the gentle rogue or the tough-guy lover—whichever the role required.

Exhaling, Jewel dropped her shoulders down an inch and let herself embrace the vision, filling herself with the essence of Taye. What a man! What temptation! But totally off-limits, too. She had to trust him and follow his direction while on the brightly lit set, but never allow the spotlight to illuminate her desire for him.

Clicking off, Jewel shut down her computer, grabbed a glass and a pitcher of iced tea from the fridge and went outside to sit by the pool. From beneath the shade umbrella on her patio, she studied the aqua-blue water, troubled by how quickly Taye Elliott had unsettled her carefully balanced emotions.

A shudder of alarm slipped through Jewel, warning her to

take control before things got too far out of hand. Surviving in Hollywood took discipline, emotional courage and the ability to shun influences that could undermine a career. Getting involved with the wrong man was certainly high on her list of things not to do.

Over the years, Jewel had dated her share of handsome, intelligent and successful men, but had never given her heart away. Perhaps her affair with the wrong man, years ago, had left her fearful of experiencing such hurt again. Now, all she wanted to do was enjoy a man's company, appreciate his attention and indulge in just enough sex to satisfy her libido without bringing him into her life, her career, her home.

Living alone made for an uncomplicated and stress-free lifestyle, guided by a simple set of rules that worked for Jewel. It was a lifestyle she'd created to survive—the one she needed and the only one she wanted. Perhaps she was so comfortable with this approach because she really didn't mind being alone. As an only child, she learned at an early age to appreciate and enjoy her own company. As a teenager back in Texas, Jewel had had little use for clubs, cliques or frivolous socialization, having carefully mapped out her plan to become a television actress, a plan she had followed with little deviation.

First, a degree in drama from the University of Texas. Next, a move to Los Angeles and more acting classes at UCLA, where she met her best friend, Marlena Kirk, who'd gotten Jewel her first important acting job. It had been a role that might have propelled Jewel straight into movie stardom if she hadn't made the mistake of falling in love with her costar, Chandler Jeffries— her mature, A-list, megastar, on-screen lover, who was married to a manipulative, influential high-profile woman.

When Jewel and Chandler's illicit relationship became public, his wife short-circuited Jewel's budding career by causing a furor of bad publicity in a public showdown in a Beverly Hills restaurant. When Chandler's wife confronted him, she forced him to dump Jewel in public and then beg her forgiveness in front of a shocked but intrigued audience.

The press had had a field day with the implosion of the scandalous love triangle, forcing Jewel into hiding to lick her wounds in shame for having been so foolish.

During this disastrous time in her life, Jewel spiraled into an emotional state that nearly paralyzed her. She couldn't work. She didn't care about her appearance. She wanted to disappear from the world. It had taken tough talk from Marlena, along with generous doses of her agent's unflagging support, to pull Jewel together and get her back into action.

Winning the female lead in *The Proud and the Passionate* had saved Jewel's career and she hoped to remain at CBC for a very long run. She hadn't become a wildly popular soap opera star by running around town with one handsome actor after another or getting romantically involved with influential producers, directors or casting agents. She had kept a low profile, refused to be sucked into the hurly-burly L.A. lifestyle where marriages crashed and burned, scandals ruined careers and hearts were broken in a casual manner. She also knew that trust was just a word and callous people had no trouble stepping on each other on their way to the top.

Now, the jarring sound of clanging bells, the new ringtone she'd downloaded last week, interrupted Jewel's mental wandering. When she saw who was calling, she grinned, stabbed Talk and said, "Hello, Marlena. I was just thinking about you. Home from church already?"

"Not yet. I'm sitting in my car, in your driveway. Wanna go to brunch at Piatto's with me? I really want to talk to you."

"Girl, please." Jewel laughed, walking around the side of her house to exit the backyard and head down the driveway where Marlena's black Lincoln Navigator SUV was parked. "You see how I'm dressed," she continued as she approached the passenger side of her agent's car and then leaned in the open window. "I have *no* plans to leave the house. Really, wish I could, but I've got a ton of things to do…pages of script to memorize. You know my Sunday drill."

Marlena leaned over and spoke through the open window.

"Do I ever. You can be such a homebody sometimes. I spend my days making sure you're the hottest actress on TV and all you want to do is cool off at home...."

"Don't start," Jewel jokingly interrupted, shaking her head. "I really don't feel like a lecture. Come on in, sit by the pool and have a glass of tea. We'll talk," Jewel invited.

"We do need to, that's for sure," Marlena agreed, turning off the engine and getting out.

While pouring a glass of iced tea for Marlena, Jewel filled her in on her accident with the van, leaving out the fact that she'd hit the vehicle because her mind had been on Taye Elliott. "Anyway," she was saying, "my car has a nasty scratch on the front bumper and I've got to put it in the shop."

"Sounds like a setup. Did you call the police?" Marlena sounded worried.

"No. The man took off, so I came on home."

"I dunno. Very strange. You did call your insurance agent and report it, I hope."

"Oh, yeah, I talked to my agent, Chuck Davies. Told me to drop off my car at the dealer Monday and after he gets an estimate for repairs, he'll call me and we'll go from there. Such a hassle. I'm just glad there wasn't any damage to the other vehicle," Jewel replied, wanting to put the nasty episode out of her mind.

"Hey, don't worry about it. West Coast Lexus will be happy to provide you with a loaner car or even a driver if you want one," Marlena advised and then added, "You know, you really should have a driver. Stop dealing with the crazies and the traffic."

Jewel laughed. "That's exactly what Carmie tells me all the time. But that's not me. I have to have my independence."

"Whatever. I'd sure take advantage of any opportunity to be chauffeured around this town." A slight huff and a pause. "Now, how'd your meeting with Taye Elliott go?"

Jewel zipped through a recap of her lunch with Fred and Taye, expressing her decision to give Taye her full support.

"I still think it's a pretty risky move on the studio's part,"

Marlena commented. "He's gotta pull out some incredible numbers to move *P & P* up during sweeps. Think he can do it?" she questioned with a snap that underscored her concern.

"Let's hope so," Jewel replied, not feeling quite as pessimistic as Marlena sounded.

"You know it's all about the money," Marlena stated with conviction. "The network wasn't going to shell out big bucks for a director the likes of Brad Fortune, so they went for a guy with no experience in daytime just to see what he's made of."

"So you think this is a test?" Jewel asked, recalling that she, too, had accused Taye of using *P & P* as his guinea pig.

"Of course it is. The man has no soap credentials and from what you just said, he only got the gig because of who he knows and probably to pay his bills until he gets another movie deal."

"Oh, I don't know about that," Jewel defended. "I think he's truly interested in daytime and doing good work, of course. He's cool…has a positive attitude that I think will go over with the cast. If we're lucky, we'll end May sweeps with some kick-butt ratings!"

Marlena arched a dark upswept eyebrow. "He'd better, because *Down for Love* is the hottest soap going and you guys are under some serious pressure to heat it up over there at *P & P.* Everyone knows Brad Fortune was the cement that held your show together. So now what's gonna happen?" Marlena wanted to know.

"Gee, thanks a lot," Jewel grumbled, squinting at her friend. "Guess I've just been background noise? A set decoration, huh?"

"That's not what I meant and you know it," Marlena protested. "I didn't mean to imply that your role in the success of *P & P* isn't important, but the show was Brad's vision from the beginning. When he agreed to leave *Talk about It* to direct *P & P,* the studio knew he'd bring in a winner and he did. Taye is an unknown quantity, so *we've* got to plan ahead."

"Plan ahead? For what?" Jewel asked, her fingers tensed around her glass.

"That's what I want to talk to you about," Marlena hinted.

"And?"

"If *P & P* doesn't earn at least a two-point increase in audience share in the next report, your show might be in trouble."

"What kind of trouble? You know something I don't?" Jewel snapped alert, eager for whatever Marlena had to say.

"Well." Marlena mulled her reply, letting a short silence hang between them. "I think it might be time for you to consider making a move."

"A move? You mean just walk away?" Jewel pressed three fingers across her lips, taking in what her agent had just said. "But I'm under contract. I can't blow that off."

"Happens all the time," Marlena calmly observed with the slightest hint of a challenge. "Rules are made to be broken in this business. I understand where you're coming from, Jewel, but at least let's talk about your options."

"Like what?" Jewel wanted to know.

"Like the fact that the producer of *Down for Love* is interested in you for a new character he plans to introduce next month. A glamorous diamond-wearing-diva role that would fit you perfectly!"

Jewel slumped back in her chaise longue. A juicy role on *DFL?* The daytime drama that had skyrocketed to the top within weeks? But *P & P* was her home. How could she consider deserting CBC at a time when the studio needed her most? "I dunno, Marlena. Don't you think things will smooth out on *P & P* once Taye gets on board and the cast gets back on track? Brad's death put off everyone."

"But what if the situation deteriorates? Advertising revenue for *P & P* is down five percent and the execs are getting nervous. You need to seriously consider exploring this role at *DFL.*"

"Marlena," Jewel started with a sigh of resignation. "I can't think about leaving *P & P* right now. I have to think about more than just myself. What about the cast? We're an ensemble. If we're slipping, then it's up to all of us to help fix it, not turn tail and run. I can't do it."

"It's your decision."

"I know. And I'm flattered by the offer, but I don't want to break my contract to take a chance on another soap." Jewel's decision was firm. "I'm betting on the loyal followers of *P & P* to hang in there and for Taye to help us make up for lost ground."

"Things in the world of daytime TV happen fast," Marlena challenged.

"I know, but I'm not worried. I have a gut feeling that I'm going to be very happy at CBC for a long time," Jewel predicted with a new surge of confidence.

And for as long as Taye Elliott is there, she thought, recalling how his big brown eyes had devoured her, undressed her and made her yearn for his touch on her skin.

"Okay, if that's what you want." Marlena stood and shouldered her purse. "Now, I've gotta go. Meet me for brunch at Piatto's next Sunday? Eleven-thirty?"

"I'll be there," Jewel promised as she walked Marlena to her car.

Returning to her seat on the patio, Jewel considered Marlena's news. The fact that another soap was interested in her was certainly intriguing, but she knew better than to get carried away by such a flattering proposal. Change was not easy. Jewel Blaine was one of the most stable, reliable artists under contract on her show and she wasn't about to toss that hard-won reputation away because ratings were in a temporary slump. She knew actors who routinely rotated from one soap opera to another, changing roles as easily as they changed hairstyles, and she certainly didn't plan to become one of them. Longevity. Stability. Respect. That was what she'd worked for, was known for, and was not about to lose.

Chapter 11

The clanging bells of Jewel's ringtone pushed Marlena's news aside. Jewel checked the phone's screen and then exhaled in surprise. But was she really surprised? Hadn't she been hoping all morning that he'd call? That he'd been thinking about her as much as she'd been thinking about him? Taye Elliott. His face danced before her eyes. Should she take the call or let voice mail kick in? Answer now or make him wait at least an hour before she got back to him ? After a nanosecond pause, Jewel pressed Talk and said, "Hello?"

"What are you having for lunch?" Taye jumped right in, sounding very sure of himself, but rushed.

Holding the phone away from her face, Jewel wrinkled her nose and counted to five. "Probably quesadillas left over from last night."

"Naw…we can do better than that."

"We?"

"Sure. You're coming to lunch with me."

"Oh, is that so? Maybe I have other plans."

"You don't. Not if you're eating leftovers."

Damn! He got me there! "But I am busy, Taye. I've got pages and pages of script to review."

"Which you can do later."

"If I go with you to lunch, I can't stay long."

"No problem. I have an appointment later today anyway, so we can slip into a restaurant, have a quick bite and then I'll bring you straight home."

"Okay, I'm gonna hold you to that." Jewel clamped her teeth together in frustration, torn between scolding him for being so presumptive and telling him how glad she was to hear his voice. Damn, she wished she wasn't tingling all over and itching to see him again. If only she could push him away with a cool, reserved comeback and tell him he'd have to wait until Monday morning if he wanted to see her again. Not to presume that she was as eager to get on a personal footing with him as he seemed to be about her. However, in an unguarded moment, her mouth took over. "Where do you want to go?"

"You choose."

Jewel scrambled to think. A place nearby. Very public. Where, if she and Taye were recognized, it would be clear that they were simply having a business lunch. "What about The Grove?" she offered. It was in the heart of L.A., crowded with locals and tourists, and not usually frequented by the paparazzi.

"What? The Grove? That tourist trap?" He sounded offended. "I was thinking of someplace nicer, quieter. Maybe drive over to the marina, find a spot where we could be more private."

"I like The Grove. I know it's kinda funky, in a hip sort of way. *National Travel* calls it one of the top ten people-watching spots in Los Angeles."

An indistinguishable mutter came to Jewel over the line. "That's what I'm afraid of," Taye complained. "People watching *us*. Tourists gawking, interrupting our meal. Do you really want to be bothered?"

"Oh, I'm used to that," Jewel tossed back lightly. "And I

know how to dodge unwanted attention when I'm out and about. I do it all the time."

"What do you have in mind? Wearing a disguise?"

"Perhaps."

"Like what? A Michael Jackson face mask?"

"No." She laughed. "Nothing that drastic. A big sun hat and large dark glasses usually do the trick."

"So, you plan to play mystery woman for me?" he softly joked. "Um. Actually, that might be quite a turn-on."

His sensual voice sent tiny vibrations through Jewel, fluttering with the beat of her heart, forcing her to wait a few seconds before speaking. "Hmm...let's not get into any thoughts of erotic role-play, all right? You're beginning to sound kinda kinky," she matched his tease, defusing the moment.

However, Taye took the bait and ran with it. "Are you telling me you don't ever conjure up wonderfully delicious but impossible scenarios in your head?"

"I'm not saying that." Jewel bit her bottom lip, knowing she had better choose her next words very carefully. "There's nothing wrong with fantasizing, as long as you remember what's out of reach, what's a figment of your imagination and what can never become real."

"Thank you for reminding me," Taye said. "But for now, can you dream up a vision of us sitting at a table in a restaurant eating Caesar salads and sipping Perrier?"

She had to laugh at the way their banter had pushed her into a more receptive mood. "Fine. I'll be ready in an hour. Big hat, dark glasses and all."

Jewel hung up, satisfied with her suggestion that they go to The Grove, an outdoorsy area of L.A. that included restaurants, theaters, a parklike setting with mall shopping and even a farmers' market featuring a massive selection of sweets, veggies and unusual ethnic food. She could not recall the last time she'd been there and the prospect of spending a few hours there with Taye might be fun.

But did she *really* want to start down this road with him?

They'd had lunch on Friday, dinner on Saturday and now lunch on Sunday afternoon.

"This is getting out of hand, Jewel," she reprimanded under her breath, ashamed that she'd so easily allowed Taye Elliott to blast a hole in her rule against crossing into personal zones with coworkers. However, sizzling with anticipation, she hurried into her bedroom, having already decided what she would wear.

Exactly one hour later, Taye was standing in the sheltered alcove at Jewel's front door, finger on the doorbell, recalling that he'd been in that very same spot less than twenty-four hours earlier. The memory of her expression when he'd touched her lips with his finger initiated a surge in his groin that took him by surprise. Not wanting his reaction to be apparent when she opened the door, he snapped to attention and fisted his hands, tamping down his runaway urges.

The front door swung open. An unexpected gasp of pleasure slipped from Taye at seeing her again. She was clearly ready to tackle The Grove where people-watching, store-hopping and browsing stalls of vegetables and flowers were major activities to pass the time. She was dressed in dark-rinse jeans, a white tank top under a fluttering black-and-white knit poncho, comfortable black flat shoes with shiny gold buckles on the toes and a mini-purse on a string hung crosswise over her chest. Her hair was a loose wave of dark ringlets and she was carrying a floppy black straw hat banded with white ribbon.

"Hello. You're a very punctual man, I see. That's nice," Jewel remarked with a tilt of her lips, stepping outside. She shoved on her dark glasses, turned and bent to lock the door.

"Timing is ingrained in my genes," Taye replied, unable to ignore the lovely curve of her prominent backside, so nicely presented to him, while extremely relieved that she hadn't invited him in. No telling what he might have done if he'd gotten her inside, because right then, eating lunch at The Grove was the last thing on his mind.

"I guess that's a huge prerequisite to being a good stuntman, huh?" she asked, turning around to face to him.

"You got that right. Missing a cue by a tenth of a second could mean injury, even death." Holding on to Jewel's arm, he walked her to his Hummer, helped her climb inside and, after buckling up, they took off toward the corner of Third and Fairfax, where The Grove sprawled out in L.A. welcome.

When Jewel picked up their conversation where she'd left it, Taye found her interest in him rather appealing. She sounded genuine, as if she truly wanted to know how he'd become who he was and what fueled his path through life.

"So," Jewel was saying, "as a kid, did you do a lot dangerous things? Like blow up mailboxes and tease rattlesnakes with sticks? Did you pretend to be Superman and jump off the roof of your garage wearing a blanket around your shoulders?"

A loud guffaw, followed by a dismissive jerk of his chin gave Jewel her answer. "Absolutely not. I wasn't into comic books and action heroes…mainly because they weren't promoted very much around my house."

"Not even GI Joe?"

"Unfortunately, no. You see, my father had this idea that if he restricted my and my brothers' toys to science kits, doctor kits, microscopes, telescopes and all things endorsed by *National Geographic,* we'd be better suited for the profession he'd chosen for us."

"He wanted his sons to be scientists?"

"No, doctors. My father is an M.D. He owns a clinic back home in Pittsburgh. The Elliott Cosmetic Surgery Center, where he and my three doctor-brothers work."

"Oh? All of your brothers are doctors? Impressive. Any sisters?"

"Nope, just us four boys. My parents divorced when I was six. Dad got custody, which was fine with my mom, who remarried and moved to Michigan. We drifted out of touch long ago."

"Gee, that's too bad. My mom is still back home in Jefferson, Texas, and we're as close as we can be under the circumstances. She's afraid of flying, so she won't visit the West Coast, but I try to get home every few years. Anyway, back to you. How'd you manage to escape going into the family business and why get involved in movies?"

"Long story," Taye said without looking over at her, sensing the intense beam of her eyes on him even though she was wearing her wraparound Chanel sunglasses. "I tried to go along with the program but just couldn't cut it. My father was furious when I dropped out of med school in my last year. My two oldest brothers, Don and William, thought I was crazy to try to get into stunt work when I could have a perfectly safe life behind a surgical mask. My younger brother, Cliff, was better about it. Think he's envious that I had the guts to stand up to my dad. Anyway, I went for the most dangerous and risky side of the movies and I got my first job." A shrug and a pause as he cut his eyes to Jewel. "Sure you want to hear all of this?"

"Of course," she tossed back, sounding sincere. "I want to get to know you, Taye. *Really* know you." Her tone had turned softly genuine. "And I'm guessing that you want to know me better, too. Am I getting the signals right?"

Taye braked at the stoplight, turned to Jewel and studied the flawless skin of her forehead, her cheeks, her neck—all dewy and soft tan in the afternoon sun. *Camera perfect,* he observed, understanding why *Soap Opera Digest* had included her in this year's list of daytime's ten most beautiful stars. And while tempted to reach over, grab her by the arm, pull her body closer to his and insist they skip lunch to feed the hunger that was growing between his legs, he simply exhaled slowly and repeated her comment. "Do I want to know you better?" A tense spark of silence. "More than you can ever imagine."

They didn't speak again until arriving at The Grove, a sprawling complex next to a historical farmers' market with a dancing fountain in front. The popular spot was crowded, and its lively streets with their old-fashioned look bustled with activity.

Taye walked easily beside Jewel past restaurants and shops,

taking care not to hold her hand or drape an arm across her shoulders or lean in too close when he turned to talk to her. Even though he desperately wanted to slip an arm around her waist in a protective, and yes, possessive, move, he managed to restrain himself.

They paused in front of the Pacific Movie Theater to look at the posters and comment on an upcoming foreign film marathon.

"I can't wait for this," she commented, pointing at a poster for a film from Spain entitled *Flores de la Luna.* "Opens next Saturday. The reviews have been fantastic."

"I know. I loved the reviewer's description of the woman who sells the flowers," Taye remarked.

"You did?" Jewel pulled back in surprise, scrutinizing Taye with an expression of disbelief. "So you like foreign films, too?"

"Love them, and this one ought to be fantastic," Taye agreed, stopping short of inviting her to see it with him, although what could be better than to sit in the dark next to her, to snuggle down to enjoy a film they both liked while sharing a huge bag of popcorn and drinking from the same straw?

Jewel tugged his arm. He gave himself a mental jerk, dissolving his fantasy moment. Walking on, they watched a choreographed water-and-music show at the elaborate fountain and tossed quarters into the water of the stunning creation from the designers of the Bellagio Hotel fountains in Las Vegas.

After visiting the magnificent glockenspiel musical clock located on the dome at the center of the complex, they decided on sushi for lunch and slipped into a quiet Japanese eatery where deep padded booths lined the walls.

While spearing California rolls and tuna maki with chopsticks, they talked about their mutual love of movies, favorite lines of dialogue, memories connected to movie events and anything but the obvious attraction that was rapidly building between them.

Taye was impressed by Jewel's knowledge of and interest in both classic and independent films, and was enraptured by her lively conversation. As he watched her talk, Taye easily pictured them together, as a couple, flying off to film festivals and indie screenings around the globe. What a partner in life she would make!

After lunch, instead of making Taye hurry to take her home, as he'd thought she would, Jewel suggested they get ice-cream cones from a street vendor and then explore the farmers' market.

He quickly agreed, eager for any extra moment he could spend with her. It had been a revealing afternoon and he was learning more about her. He was beginning to anticipate her facial reactions, to read her body language, to decipher which buttons to push or not, to get the emotion he wanted and would eventually need on camera. The better he knew her, the better he'd be able to direct her, but the last thing he wanted was for Jewel to feel unsure of his ability to be both her friend and her director. What he wanted was her trust.

They caught the electric-powered trolley car that linked the entertainment center to the farmers' market, even though it was hardly necessary to take the train to travel the short three-block distance. As the cheerful green car took off, Taye slipped his hand into Jewel's, enjoying the funky, homey outing and not wanting it to end.

When Jewel took Taye's hand in hers, she felt him relax, confirming her suspicion that he'd been struggling not to touch her ever since he picked her up. As the little trolley chugged along, she pressed her shoulder into his, as if thanking him for being so politely attentive all afternoon and for treating her with respect, as if they were teenagers on their first date.

First date? What was she thinking? Quickly, Jewel eased her hand from Taye's and grabbed hold of the shiny chrome pole in front of her, staring straight ahead. Had she just mentally referred to this spontaneous, friendly outing as a date? *Don't be stupid,* she cautioned, relieved when the trolley lurched to a stop and everyone clamored to get off.

While exploring the farmers' market, she kept up her guard, too, making sure there was no less than six inches of space between them. When they returned to his car, she insisted on climbing in unassisted, as if afraid of what might happen if she surrendered to his touch. However, her vigilance wavered when he pulled to a stop at her front door and she was unable to stop herself from committing the mistake she'd vowed not to make. She asked him if he wanted to come inside.

"Wish I could, but no. I have to be somewhere in about an hour," he told her, sounding rather cool.

Jewel felt like a fool for having asked. She should have known he'd keep his distance just to prove that he had more self-discipline than her. "Sure. Well, I had a…" she started, wanting to thank him for a wonderful afternoon. However, before she could finish her sentenced Taye slid across the seat, bringing his lips to her cheek.

Jewel quickly opened the passenger-side door, jumped down and hurried toward her front door.

Taye got out and followed.

Jewel watched him approach, resting her head against her front door.

He pressed in closer and smothered her lips with his in the long-awaited kiss she'd been wishing for all afternoon. Greedily, she savored the lingering hint of chocolate-mint ice cream as his tongue explored and tested and teased hers with an explosive mixture of subtle caution and driven desire. Electrified by this intimate connection, she gripped his arms and urged him closer, while knowing she ought to be pulling away.

Taye felt only the hint of a struggle before Jewel relaxed and slipped forward, her firm, high breasts pressing his chest, her thighs molding hotly with his. Slowly, cautiously, he eased one hand along her back, hesitating at the edge of her sweater, unsure of how far he dared to go and wondering why in the world he was even pushing Jewel this way after the promise he'd so boldly made.

When Jewel's tongue sweetly stroked his, he knew he was lost. Either he went the rogue route and took her inside and made love to her right then, or he backed off and walked away, keeping his gentleman's reputation intact. A flash of sanity crashed into his mind, illuminating his only choice. Taye let his hand drop away, stepped back a few inches and gazed down at Jewel with a small groan of regret.

"Not a good idea, huh?" he whispered in a voice raw with longing.

"No, it isn't. This is way off the chart, Taye. Crazy, in fact," Jewel concurred, her gaze traveling over his face, making him want her all the more.

How could he disagree? Wrong? Crazy? Impossible? Yes! But he couldn't help himself. What was it about this woman that made him want to take such chances? What he wanted most right then was to remain in her arms all night and awaken to feel her next to him in the morning.

"Crazy, for sure," he lamely repeated, yearning to kiss her until his lips were numb, until he'd had his fill of the delicious berry-sweet essence of her lipstick, until he was totally immersed in her soul.

Rashly, Taye resumed kissing her, moving from the side of her neck to trace his tongue over her ear and then nuzzle her throat. Instantly, he grew as hard and firm as the green cucumbers they'd jokingly admired at the farmers' market. When he inched his palm along her thigh, she rose to meet his touch, a muted growl of pleasure coming from her throat, followed by the press of her hands on his chest.

"Taye…whew! Wait a minute." She shifted deeper into the alcove. He moved in tandem with her. "We've got to stop this," she said. "Do you realize that we've already broken our promise to treat each other as coworkers and not create a messy situation?"

"Yeah, we're not doing so good in the keeping-it-just-friends department, are we?" He chuckled and then edged his lips along the hollow of her neck before planting several wet kisses beneath her chin.

"No, not good at all," she conceded in a mumble against his skin, her protest too weak to make him stop.

Lunging forward, Jewel sank against Taye and spoke to him across his shoulder. "Tell me why should I ever trust you again? Or trust myself, for that matter?"

Taye smiled to hear her voice sounding jagged with emotion and crackling with passion, revealing the depth of her emotions. Slowly, Taye maneuvered back to look into her eyes, deep brown pools of arousal that fueled the stir between his legs— soulfully, sinfully drawing him toward that point of no return.

"I promise you can trust me never to hurt you," he said.

"But how can I be sure?"

"Because I'm totally in tune with you," he answered in rasping words spoken without caution.

"How do you know that?"

"Instinct. Timing. A matter of judgment." His reply was serious, almost stern. "Believe me, Jewel. I won't steer you wrong. Not on the set or off. You can trust me to do what's right." Taking a short step backward, he loosened his touch and let Jewel slip away.

Sniffing softly, she crossed her arms loosely at her waist, head to one side as she considered his remark. "That's asking an awful lot, Taye, and on such short notice, too."

"Not really," Taye defended. "Not if you're as smart as I think you are and as ready to be loved as you appear to be."

Chapter 12

The parking garage at the Century Plaza building was full, as Taye had suspected it might be on a Monday morning. Spiraling down the exit ramp, he looked at the clock in the dash of his Hummer as he sped across the street toward a surface parking lot. He was already four minutes late for his nine o'clock appointment and knew he'd have to hurry if he expected to see his attorney before he left for court. Taye pulled into the first empty space he saw, jammed a five-dollar bill into the appropriate slot and dashed across the street, praying Vincent Torini hadn't left.

"Vince, I'm so glad I caught you," Taye told his attorney, entering the lawyer's office, slightly out of breath.

"No court today. You're lucky. Sit down."

Taye sat down on the edge of a blue upholstered chair, as if poised to run off at any minute. "Well, is it over?" Taye asked, tightening his jaw as he watched for a reaction from his attorney.

"Yes…now that I have both of your signatures on the petition," Vince assured his client. "Looks like this is finally settled."

Vincent Torini was a rotund man with jet-black hair, a swarthy complexion and a thick mustache that curled up at the ends. Although he looked old-fashioned in his starched white shirt, red suspenders and blue striped bow tie, he was one of the most aggressive, high-profile divorce attorneys in the state, with a Hollywood client list that was very impressive.

"What's next?" Taye asked.

"I file the petition with the court, then you two show up and the judge declares your divorce final."

"Do I have to appear?" Taye wanted to know, dreading a face-to-face with his soon-to-be ex-wife, who had deliberately dragged their divorce proceedings out for nearly two years. He was exhausted from all the haggling between lawyers, the unnecessary stalls that had cost him plenty. He had no desire to ever see Rona Eaton again.

"Well, you don't *have* to appear," Vince replied with a nonchalant shrug. "But I would if I were you. There can always be surprises, you know? And remember, Rona went for the best she could afford when she retained Ruth Hardwick as her attorney. That woman knows her way around the law."

"Okay. I get it. So, when do you think my case will come up before the judge?"

Vince shoved a pair of black-rimmed glasses over intensely dark eyes, flipped through the pages of an official-looking document and traced lines of dense text with his index finger. "Three weeks, if we're lucky," he decided. "Huge backlog in divorce court right now."

"Well, it can't be soon enough. Rona got what she wanted…half of everything," Taye commented, relieved that the bickering was over, but angry at what he'd had to give up to end twenty-two months of negotiations.

"You played it right, Taye. You've been more than fair with Rona and this thing needed to be settled."

"Did the right thing? I guess so," Taye remarked with a touch of sarcasm. "I gave Rona damn good alimony so she could live in style. I gave her cash to buy that restaurant in North

Hollywood. And now, I've agreed to sell my ranch. Why does doing the right thing feel so wrong?"

"I understand, but the law is on her side," Vince said. "The party with less support must be given a chance to get on her feet."

"But I can't believe her restaurant isn't turning a profit by now." Taye shook his head in frustration, dumbfounded that after all he'd done to help Rona start over, she was still bleeding him dry.

Vince reached for a folder, opened it and took out a stack of papers. "I reviewed her last tax return and her financial records for the past eighteen months," Vince said. "It's all here. Rona's restaurant is heavily in the red. Looks like it'll be a while before your ex sees any profit from that venture."

"And because Rona's still in debt, my ranch has to go up for sale. Not exactly the way I wanted things to go."

"I know, but helping her finance the restaurant was a smart move, Taye. In the long run, she'll become financially secure and you won't feel like you kicked her to the curb. You know what I mean? Divorce is never a cut-and-dry affair. Somebody always has to give up more than the other and as for having to sell the ranch, well, Taye, that's California law. You bought Double Pass while you were married to Rona, it's community property, so she gets half so she can support herself until her business makes money." Vincent made his comments with the somber assessment of an experienced divorce attorney who had been down this path many times before.

"I hate like hell that I gotta sell Double Pass." Taye's remark was resolute and hard. "Rona visited the ranch only once, spent the night and hated every minute. Too far from the city. Too isolated and crude for her taste. When I bought that land, she agreed that it'd be my retreat. Mine. I built it out of nothing."

"Puttin' it on the market was the only way you were gonna get Rona to sign, so think about the upside. You're home free now...and you can stop running up my bill."

Taye didn't laugh at Vince's attempt to joke about the huge fees he was charging for his services. For nearly two years Taye had been shelling out big bucks in a money-draining no-win battle to get rid of Rona Eaton, the attractive underemployed actress he'd met and mistakenly married four years ago after too many mai tais and piña coladas at a chance encounter in the Tiki Lounge of the Palace Hotel on Sunset Strip.

They met during the wrap party for a movie in which he'd stunt doubled for Will Smith. They hooked up, got a room and engaged in mind-blowing sex, a satisfying end to the dry spell he'd endured during his remote location shoot. Instantly inseparable, he and Rona spent most of their time either tumbling around his king-size bed or planning their next sexual encounter, and within a month they were living together in Taye's condominium in Thousand Oaks.

Their steamy escapades clouded Taye's judgment about as much as their soapy sex clouded the walls of his multijet shower. Blinded by Rona's seductive largess, Taye let her lead him into a civil marriage ceremony where he eagerly said, "I do," and put a huge pink diamond on Rona's finger.

At the time, marrying Rona Eaton had seemed like a natural progression of their hot-and-heavy relationship. Taye was horny, hunky and easy to please. Rona was gorgeous, exciting, playful and sexually adventurous in ways any man could only dream about.

However, soon after the rings had been exchanged and the knot had been tied, Taye realized that he'd made a huge mistake. Rona was a compulsive shopper, buying everything from boxes of tissue to Jimmy Choo shoes, making serious inroads into Taye's bank account. When he bought four hundred acres of undeveloped land nestled in the foothills of the San Gabriel Mountains, she begged him to buy her a multimillion-dollar house in Beverly Hills because, after all, he was in the movies and had an obligation to look successful. Taye quickly nixed that idea. Rona called him a selfish bastard and threatened to leave.

Everything went downhill after that. They split up. Taye gave her his condo, where Rona still lived, and moved to his ranch, sixty-three miles from Los Angeles. It was his escape, where Taye could play real-life cowboy and be alone with his horses and hay.

"Well, I've gotta get to the studio," he muttered to Vince, shaking off memories just as his attorney's desk phone rang.

"Wanna stick around while I give the clerk a call to see if I can get a better fix on a court date?" Vince asked.

"No," Taye decided. "Can't do that now. I've gotta be at CBC in fifteen minutes. But if you hear anything I need to know, call me on my cell and leave a message."

Driving away from his attorney's office, Taye wanted to feel good about what had just transpired but didn't. He was angry at himself for failing at matrimony. He'd gone for sex and excitement instead of marrying a woman he could love forever, who wanted to be his partner as they created a family and a future together. *Would he ever have that?* he worried, swallowing the bitter taste that the whole affair still left in his mouth.

The blame was mostly his, not Rona's. He'd known exactly who she was, but he'd been restless, lonely and willing to take a chance on a woman who'd made him feel good, with whom he'd had very little in common and barely known.

When the exit sign for Victoria Street caught his eye, Taye swerved onto the off-ramp, deciding to see for himself just how Simply Delicious, Rona's restaurant in North Hollywood, was doing. He pulled into the parking lot on the side of the shop, surprised to find it nearly full. Getting out, he went over to the large front window and looked inside. Taye checked his watch. Nine-fifty in the morning. A pretty big crowd for so early in the morning. What kind of a crowd would be there for lunch? Dinner? he wondered as he returned to his car. *Simply Delicious looks like it's doing pretty well.… Well enough for Rona to support herself without money from me.*

Driving away, Taye felt anger building in his chest. Rona had what she wanted, while he had to put up his ranch for sale. But what did he expect from a woman whose main goal in marrying him had been to take as much as she could? Working as a stunt double on action films had been hard, bruising work, but it had also paid extremely well, providing Taye with the kind of life-style that had attracted Rona's attention. She'd viewed him as her opportunity to latch on to an authentic connection to the movie industry and create a shortcut to stardom for herself.

Well, he was finally free. *Or am I?* he worried, concerned that his emotions were all tangled up again—with a woman who should definitely be off-limits. *Why am I getting into another impossibly complicated relationship? What's the matter with me?* he asked himself, knowing the answer. *Jewel Blaine, that's what.*

Taye's attraction to Jewel was intense, filling him with a smothering closeness that created a catch in his breath just to think about her. He'd decided that it was the kind of over-whelming reaction that must come from falling in love: an intense longing that he'd never experienced with Rona, who had been readily available and too easily accommodated.

Jewel was different: approachable, yet distant. Professional, but passionate. Demanding of respect while sending teasing signals to keep him unsure enough to stick around. As much as Taye wanted to remain cool and friendly in his relationship with Jewel, he knew his feelings for her were rapidly spiraling out of control and he was reluctant to rein them in.

A smile flitted across Taye's lips to recall how good she'd felt in his arms when he'd kissed her yesterday. It had been a risky move, but it had also told him what he wanted to know. They shared a chemistry that could easily explode into some-thing very special. She was gutsy enough to accept his chal-lenge and wanted him as much as he wanted her. But was he willing to show enough restraint to play it slow with her?

Taye knew he didn't dare plunge headfirst into this adven-ture, because Jewel was a woman who moved with caution. While he didn't care if the whole world knew how attracted he was to her, he didn't want to frighten her or make her feel uneasy at the studio.

But is it really the threat of workplace gossip that makes her so cautious? Could she have another man in her life? Someone who would not appreciate her interest in me? Why not? Certainly a woman as beautiful and talented as Jewel Blaine must have tons of men clamoring for her attention. How could he fault her for wanting to maintain control of her privacy while living such a public life?

Taye was in the business. He understood the pressures that actors faced. Working as a stunt double had allowed him the luxury of being in the movies without the hassles than came with celebrity. His work had trained him to be confident, positive and unafraid of taking chances. Well, pursuing Jewel Blaine was certainly taking a chance, but one thing was clear: as her director, he couldn't avoid being around her, so he'd just have to play the situation as she wanted for now and see how far she would let him go.

Inching along the 405 in midmorning traffic, Taye let his thoughts slip back to the first real risk he'd ever taken—the one he still worked hard to prove: dropping out of his last year of medical school to move to L.A. to pursue an acting career. However, if that hadn't happened, he never would have gone into directing, never would have been hired to direct *P & P* and never would have had a reason to get this close to Jewel Blaine.

Chapter 13

The conference room door swung open as *P & P*'s head writer, Lori Callyer, rushed in, looking frazzled and out of breath. She was slender, with tendrils of yellow-gold hair exploding from a red clip on top of her head. The resolute set to her jaw was softened by the sheen of ambition in her sparkling green eyes. Lori, who was jokingly referred to as Ms. Rapid Writer because of the impromptu script changes she could be counted on to make in the middle of a shoot, greeted her colleagues with a choppy wave and a jangle of thin silver bracelets. "Sorry I'm late. Had to get these last-minute changes on paper for you guys."

"More changes? Aw, really?" Barbara and Janie Olden, the twins who played Darin Saintclare's nosy neighbors, piped up in unison. Others sitting around the black lacquer table groaned, knowing this meant even more time in the read-through than previously scheduled.

Lori shot an I-dare-you-to-complain look at the actors who brought her words to life. "Only six pages. Not so much and we'll get started as soon as Taye gets here…. He called from his car. Should be pulling into the parking garage right now."

Jewel slipped lower in her seat and took a sip from the cup of herbal tea she'd brought to the Monday-morning read-through. With a quick scan, she took note of those already assembled at the table: her leading man, Sonny Burton. The essence of mahogany cool. Six foot two, fine enough to make the cover of *Male Model* magazine three times and the man Jewel counted among her short list of close friends. She probably would have fallen in love with Sonny if he hadn't already been happily married to a woman Jewel admired, with five sons, all of whom looked like carbon copies of their father.

Next to Sonny was Karen Adams, the second-tier producer who was sitting in for Fred Warner. Technical director Alana Broadnax, who worked closely with Taye, sat across from Richard Young, head of advertising and sales, and a man who rarely attended routine read-throughs. *Probably because of the P& P ratings war with* Down for Love, Jewel calculated, knowing how closely advertising revenue was tied to ratings, which were tied to production, which started and ended with the story line and the actors, etc., etc., etc.

Lori continued to hand out stapled sheaves of paper until Taye entered the room. He was accompanied by a raven-haired young woman whose black knit sweater was clearly two sizes too small and who was wearing gold hoop earrings too large for her face.

"Hi, Taye. Hi, Suzy. Right on time. We're just about ready to get started," Lori breezily greeted.

"Fine," Taye replied, passing three empty chairs to take a seat directly across from Jewel, who nodded at him and then turned her attention to Suzy Rabu. The dark-haired Pakistani beauty with dimples the size of quarters had been Brad Fortune's right-hand woman. Jewel watched with interest as Suzy went to the refreshment table, poured black coffee into a CBC mug, added a dash of cream and then handed it to Taye, who grinned his thanks at her.

So, Suzy already knows how Taye takes his coffee, Jewel observed, straightening her back and jerking her eyes off the woman. She began paging mindlessly through her script, aware that Taye was watching, and mildly irritated that he'd made it a point to sit where he could stare at her. *He's testing me. Wants to see how I'll react to him in this setting,* she decided, determined to treat him with cool respect—as if he'd never come to dinner at her house, had never kissed her against her wishes. As if she had never kissed him back.

When her BlackBerry buzzed, Jewel checked the screen and saw that West Coast Lexus was calling. The meeting was not yet under way; she had a few minutes, so she got up and ducked into a corner of the conference room to take the call.

Frowning, Jewel listened as the manager of the Lexus dealership informed her that the damage to her car was much more extensive than she had thought. The underpinning support bars behind the front bumper were twisted and it would take at least two or three days to get the parts, fixing it at a cost of thirty-seven hundred dollars! Also, her insurance agent, Chuck Davies, wanted to speak with her right away. He had some questions to ask her before he would authorize payment.

"Don't worry about the money," Jewel advised, irritated by this unwanted development. "I'll give Mr. Davies a call and work out the details. Just put the deductible on my credit card and get started with the repairs," Jewel advised with annoyance. This should be a routine repair job. She didn't have time to dicker with Statewide Insurance over a simple collision claim. She'd told Davies when she'd spoken to him Saturday that she had been at fault, that there'd been no damage to the vehicle she'd hit. Why couldn't he just dispense the funds she'd so diligently paid his company over the past five years and fix the damn car?

Jewel clamped her lips together in frustration, firmly convinced that Chuck Davies, a soft-spoken man with a tinny voice, was deliberately making this process more of a hassle than it had to be to flex his authority. Well, she had work to do, a read-through to perform and too much on her mind to get into a rehash of her accident right then. She'd call Davies after the meeting broke up.

With a jab of her finger, Jewel shut off her phone and returned to her seat, shaking her head in disbelief.

Taye leaned over and whispered, "Anything wrong?"

Jewel thumbed the space between her brows, trying to tamp down her irritation. "Yeah. My car. They've gotta replace the bumper and some connecting rods. A lot more damage than I thought. It's gonna take a few more days."

"Too bad. If you want a second opinion, I can give you the name of my mechanic."

"No. I don't. Thank you very much."

"Guess you'll need a ride home, then?" he prompted conspiratorially, a sly grin tugging at his upper lip.

A curt shake of her head. "No. I don't. I can call for a car," she whispered back.

"But why ride home with a stranger when I'm available?"

"I'll bet you are. I can handle this, okay?"

"If you change your mind, let me know."

"I won't."

"Well, if I can do *anything,* you know I'm here."

Jewel shot Taye a scolding glance, silently rebuking his double entendres. "You need to stop," she hissed, trying to sound annoyed while smothering a bubble of laughter. As she held his eyes with hers, everyone in the room faded away. She was alone with Taye, in the alcove at her front door, his lips blissfully searching hers in hungry exploration. A hint of wetness dampened her white lace panties. Blood rushed to her head. Jewel swiveled in her chair and turned her back on Taye, nervous about the erotic visions crowding in.

What is it with this man? He is absolutely incorrigible! I will not leave the studio with him no matter how much he presses the offer. Jewel Blaine and Taye Elliott zooming off together in his Hummer? Wouldn't that be good fodder for water-cooler gossip tomorrow?

Jewel sank back in relief when Lori tapped Taye on the shoulder. "Ready to get started?"

"Oh. Yeah," he answered, looking up at Lori, who introduced and officially welcomed Taye to CBC.

After a round of applause and everyone had settled down, Taye made a short speech, telling everyone how pleased he was to be at CBC, adding more about his background. From the hoots of appreciation when he mentioned his work on the *Terror Train* series, it was obvious that he had many fans in the room.

"So, here I am, ready to get to work, and I plan to move quickly, guys, because we've got a lot to do. Get prepared for a very long day," Taye warned. "I understand how difficult Brad's death has been on everyone. My goal is to keep *P & P* as fresh and hot as he did. Now, let's pick up the story line on page fifteen, then we'll block out the next twenty pages."

Jewel nodded her agreement, while Sonny Burton gave Taye a quick thumbs-up, bobbing his head in the affirmative.

"Lori's given you the new script," Taye continued. "She and I met briefly late yesterday evening and made a few changes that we'll run through now, just so everyone understands the shift in direction."

Jewel twitched, stunned to hear that Taye and Lori had gotten together on Sunday evening. After he'd left her house. Why hadn't he told her he was meeting with Lori? What had he been trying to hide?

Jewel swung her gaze toward Taye, but he ignored her, got up and walked to the front of the room. He was wearing a soft blue denim shirt with the sleeves rolled up to his elbows, unbuttoned just enough to expose a few inches of his deeply tanned chest. Stonewashed jeans hugged his muscled thighs and defined his hard, tan body. Today, his hair—a soft jumble of black curls that caressed the rim of his shirt collar—was not as carefully combed as it had been on Sunday and the slightly messy look added a sexy edge to his appearance. She suppressed a smile, liking what she saw, but not totally sold on Taye, who definitely had an agenda that he did not plan to share with her.

"We've received a deluge of correspondence from fans who've been quick to inform us that they're sick of reruns and ready for Darin Saintclare and Caprice Desmond to get back to the showdown that was put on hold," Taye went on.

"So true," Suzy piped up. "And FYI, everybody…each e-mail gets an answer." She started scrolling through the *P & P* Web site on the laptop computer she was never without. A major part of Suzy's job was to keep her finger on the pulse of the public to see how various plotlines or episodes did or did not fly. "We use a standard auto-reply to acknowledge most e-mails, but sometimes, if the message warrants, I send a few personalized lines.… Some fans deserve a bit more attention."

"Good public relations," Taye replied. "Okay, let's start on page fifteen." Moving around the table as the reading proceeded, Taye listened closely, interrupting actors to clarify his interpretation of a scene or answer a question about timing. Taye's supportive attitude infused Jewel with a heightened sense of respect. He was saying precisely the right things to the cast and in the right tone, winning everyone over with his easy-going yet focused style.

Smart man, she decided, appreciating the smooth manner in which he was handling what could have been an uneasy transition and impressed by how prepared he was. He was confident, relaxed and truly interested in hearing what the cast had to say and he certainly knew how to manage.

As the read-through came to Jewel's lines, Taye eased his way toward her. She tensed, flubbing a line when he stopped so close to her that his thigh nearly grazed her shoulder. *Is anyone else bothered by his citrus-fresh scent?* she wondered, his heart-tugging aroma filling her head, unsettling her nerves and distracting her as much as it had Sunday night. Taking a calming breath, she started over and made it through the scene.

Finished with her lines, Jewel placed her script on the table with a soft slap, rotated her neck and raised her chin, desperate to ignore Taye's close proximity and forget about the memory of the velvety touch of his lips on hers. It had all been a joke, hadn't it? A silly way to cap off their day at The Grove and make a point of defusing the sexual tension that was rapidly building. *Forget about it,* she told herself, exhaling under her breath. *I'm here to work, not fantasize about a man I can never have. But once he's finished with* P & P, *maybe…*

"Now, Sonny," Lori was saying, pulling Jewel back to the meeting. "I want you to let Jewel carry the argument. Engage her and then back off so she can go after you."

"Got it," Sonny agreed, making a note in the margin of his script before turning to Jewel. "Whata you think? Makes sense to me. With all the people standing around the hotel lobby watching us fight, it'll make Darin even more uncomfortable when you go ballistic."

Jewel just stared at Sonny, mouth open.

"Whata you think, Jewel?" he prodded.

Jolted alert, she narrowed her eyes at her costar. "Think about what? What argument in what hotel lobby?" she sputtered, embarrassed to have blanked out and missed an important exchange.

Lori appraised Jewel with wide eyes. "I cut the beach scene and moved the argument to the hotel lobby."

"Oh?" Jewel thumbed through the script, found the scene change, scanned her lines and then screwed her mouth to one side, thinking. "But this is supposed to be on the beach. Moving it inside changes the tone completely, Lori." She shot a hard look at Taye. "I thought we were going to reshoot the beach scene on Catalina."

"I changed my mind," Taye clarified. "Lori and I decided that there's no time for a complicated location shoot. It'll work fine in the hotel." He bent over the table and presented Jewel with a satisfied smile.

Caught off guard, she tensed, not about to buy into his charming ploy again. Hadn't he told her that the tone of the exchange on the beach scene wouldn't change, only the location? "I'm just surprised, that's all," she finished, not wanting to make a big deal of the fact that they had worked together at her house over the weekend, that he'd told her one thing but was doing another.

"Yeah…I made the suggestion. Lori agreed. And she's the head writer."

Lori nodded smugly, sending her golden curls bouncing.

Jewel shifted in her seat, sealing the exchange with a flip of her shoulder, not about to argue the point. Lori and Taye had every right to make any changes they wanted and she had no say in the script. "Fine. Let's hope it works as well."

"I'm sure it will," Taye quickly responded, tucking the script pages in question under his folder. "Now, let's run through the scene. Sonny, Jewel, you're on. Come on up so we can get a feel for the body language."

Jewel pushed back her chair and stood, eyes wide, ears alert, not about to be blindsided again and no longer confused about Taye Elliott. Apparently, he had no problem telling her one thing in private and doing the opposite in public. At least she knew what she was dealing with now.

The room grew quiet as Jewel and Sonny proceeded to rehearse the hotel lobby scene. As the dialogue unfolded, Jewel *became* her character. She pushed Caprice to the limits, determined to make Darin understand what she wanted and what she would not tolerate. As Jewel fell deeper into her role, she lost all awareness of her surroundings, having transported herself mentally and emotionally into the fictional world of Elm Valley.

However, when Taye called out, "Stop right there," she blinked and then shot him a puzzled look.

Taye strode toward her. "Something's wrong," he said.

"What? I thought it was going fine," Jewel replied, trying to sweeten her tone, although irritated by his interruption. She and Sonny were pros. They knew what worked and so far, the scene had gelled.

"Your reaction to Darin in that last exchange was too controlled," Taye decided, pushing a clump of black hair from his forehead.

Jewel tensed, immediately offended. Taye Elliott was a

novice director with a hell of a lot to prove and she had played Caprice Desmond for years. *What did he know about her character?* she thought, wanting to challenge him in front of the cast. However, Jewel knew that would be the wrong thing to do. Taye *was* in charge, so she'd keep a cool head and not say anything she might regret.

Focusing her famous brown eyes on Taye, she boldly demanded his attention by keeping her features in as serene a mask as she could muster, determined not to let her irritation show. Why get all flustered and emotional over Taye's lame attempt to show off? She'd save her emotions for Caprice…and for the cameramen who would capture her performance and turn it into gold.

"I want you to be angry but not gushing. Don't overplay the emotion now."

Jewel swallowed the flip remark that burned the tip of her tongue and threatened to fly from her lips. This was a deliberate test to see how she'd react. *First, he says he wants Caprice to be more aggressive. Now, he says I'm overplaying the scene. What the hell does he think he can tell me about Caprice Desmond that I don't already know?* After all, she had practically created the character from scratch. Caprice was a savvy sister who had clawed her way into the power structure of Elm Valley to become the first African-American woman on the city council, poised to run for the state legislature. One day, she'd be powerful, influential and wealthy. She could not allow Darin, her on-screen lover, to put her in a position to risk everything she'd achieved just to make him look good.

"Fine," Jewel remarked, resigned.

"Good," Taye replied. "Caprice and Darin are lovers. Convince me you still love him, even though you disagree, okay?"

Jewel's resentment lodged in her throat, keeping her from saying something nasty. She ran her tongue over her pouty red lips and then turned to Sonny Burton. "You okay with this?"

"I agree with Taye. I understand what he's after," Sonny answered in an accommodating tone.

Although Jewel appreciated her costar's attempt to ratchet down the tension that was obviously growing between herself and Taye, she resented Sonny's subtle manipulation of a fight that belonged to her. She studied the script for a moment, then curved her lips into a sly smile. Jewel Blaine was a trouper and she planned to give Taye Elliott whatever he wanted.

"Why don't *you* run through this section with me, Taye?" she challenged in a sugary voice. "Show me what you're after." She fastened a riveting dare of a stare on Taye, who immediately came toward her.

"Good idea," he agreed, taking Sonny's place and easily launching the first line in the scene. "Come home with me. Tonight, Caprice," he said, opening his arms, inviting his lover in.

Jewel stepped into his embrace and clasped both hands behind his neck, preparing to deliver a snappy comeback that would demonstrate her spunk, while showing a touch of vulnerability.

"No. Not tonight, Darin. You know that's impossible!" Her words were emphatically delivered, but toned down to the level Taye wanted.

"Nothing's impossible, Caprice. Not…not if you love me," Taye continued, without reading from the script.

Jewel felt her composure begin to crack. He was talking directly to her, without referring to the pages in his hand, as if they were alone.

"Don't you dare go there, Darin." Jewel picked up her line, only half listening to herself. "How can you question my feelings for you? You know I love you, but I won't let you force me into doing something I just can't do right now." She slipped her clasped hands down to Taye's waist, resting them at the base of his spine as she caught his gaze and delivered her next line. "You know me, Darin. You understand me…and you know how I feel, don't you?" Her heart was jerking, her throat was dry and her mind was quickly going blank as she struggled to maintain the curt edge to her dialogue that Taye was after.

She watched Taye study her with steadfast clarity while the air between them vibrated. "Yes. I understand you, Caprice, and

I'm not questioning your love for me. But I...I don't know why you're being so difficult. If only..." Taye broke off in midsentence as if he'd lost his place.

Jewel started to throw him his line, but stopped, realizing what had happened.

He leaned back from Jewel, but did not refer to the script in his hand. Instead, he remained very still, as if he had no intention of leaving the circle of her arms.

Jewel blinked nervously at Taye, bit her bottom lip and then said, "I think we need a break." Her voice was brittle and uneven.

"Sure," he agreed, pushing away.

Jewel glanced at her colleagues, who were staring at her and Taye, totally caught up in what had unfolded.

"Okay, everybody. That's it!" Lori called out, breaking the awkward silence that filled the conference room. She waved her script in the air to get the cast's attention. "Fifteen-minute break and then we shoot the scene with the twins. Barbara and Janie. Stage three, set four, you're up next. Jewel, Sonny. You're finished for now. You can go relax and rehearse until later."

"Thank God," Jewel breathed in a low voice, hoping no one had heard her. She stepped away from Taye and without another word, left the conference room, glad to get away from him if only for an hour.

Chapter 14

As soon as Jewel closed the door to her dressing room, she called West Coast Lexus and reserved a car to pick her up at eight-thirty, having already been warned that the cast would be working late.

Next, she placed a call to Chuck Davies at Statewide Insurance, but his secretary advised Jewel that he'd been called to San Diego for an emergency hearing on a case and would get back to her tomorrow. Annoyed, yet somewhat relieved to put off dealing with him, Jewel turned her attention to her wardrobe, which was hanging on the clothes rack near the door: navy linen slacks, a white satin camisole, a spiffy red blazer to top it off. Coordinated jewelry, shoes and purse were positioned on the upper shelf of the clothes rack.

Stepping out of her jeans and blouse, Jewel slipped into her black silk makeup robe, ready for Shana to arrive and perform her magic. Sitting at her makeup table, she began to use the wait time to go over her lines.

While reviewing the hotel lobby scene, she had to admit that

Lori had done a great job of defining the on-air couple's bristly relationship. Standing, Jewel began to pace her dressing room, feeling the scene and speaking her dialogue as if she were talking directly to Darin Saintclare. This was how she routinely prepared before a shoot, but today, nothing seemed routine. She felt anxious, jittery and apprehensive—sensations she'd never experienced so acutely before.

Was she nervous because of the changes in the script? Because she missed Brad Fortune, whose presence had been so reassuring? Or were her panties in a knot because of Taye Elliott and the rocketing emotions he'd stirred?

Unable to concentrate, Jewel tossed her script aside and slumped down on the blue-and-white-striped love seat at the far end of her dressing room. Thinking back over the morning meeting, she realized how easily Taye had won the trust and respect of Lori as well as the rest of the cast.

As easily as he won me over, she concluded, unable to get him out of her head. She'd blurred the lines between her personal and professional relationship with Taye. She shouldn't have invited him to her house when they could have met at a restaurant. Why had she agreed to flit around The Grove with him on Sunday when she could have stayed at home? Why had she deliberately complicated everything by kissing him back when she should have pushed him away?

Touching her bottom lip, Jewel made a little shiver, both incensed and stirred by the fact that Taye made her tingle all over. Yes, she liked him. Probably too much. And as improbable as it seemed, she was seriously thinking of going full speed ahead to explore whatever was drawing her into Taye's seductive charms.

How can something so deliciously wonderful be bad for me? she pondered. What would her colleagues at *P & P* think if she entered into a sexual relationship with their director? Would they treat her differently? Resent her? Exclude her from their bitch sessions in the lunchroom where everyone felt free to vent about the studio, the story line and even the director? Hold back from doing their best work?

The last thing Jewel wanted was to become a disruptive influence on the set. However, she could not suppress her growing need to be with Taye.

Maybe if I'm very careful, I can pull it off. If I can treat Taye with polite respect while we're working and be cautious about our public appearances, no one need know what we do in private.

The possibility began to work its way into Jewel's mind with an insistent curiosity. How ironic was it that on television, she played Caprice Desmond, a complicated diva who flaunted her romantic escapades, while in fact, Jewel Blaine was worried about keeping romance at arm's length.

In public statements, Jewel took great care to refer to herself as a happily single woman with no desire to complicate her life with a husband, a long-term lover or even children. However, Jewel could not deny that she'd love nothing better than a romantic relationship with an attentive man and a raucous large family who would embrace her with love.

But did Taye Elliott fit that role? Was he the one destined to play that part in her life? she worried.

When Jewel signed her first contract with CBC, she created a game plan for success: no romantic entanglements with married men, costars, producers or directors. Hollywood was a place where people traveled in small circles and gossip traveled faster than cars racing along the 405. The more distance she kept between her professional world and her private life, the better off she was. Media pressure, jealousy, backbiting and ambition could ruin a career, destroy a relationship and dim the brilliance of promise. She'd been through that once before and wasn't going there again.

A fast triple-knock on her dressing room door brought Jewel's mental plotting to a stop. She adjusted her robe and then called out, "Come on in, Shana! I'm ready."

But when Jewel glanced up, she saw her executive director, not her makeup artist, standing at the entry, his head slanted to one side, studying her with a tentative expression.

This man is too damn smooth, she couldn't help but think as she watched him standing there, solemn-faced, as if asking for permission to come in. His eyes seemed to be pleading for understanding, his lips begging for forgiveness, while his body-builder physique sizzled beneath his clothes.

"Well, don't just stand there gawking, come on in," she invited in a voice she struggled to steady.

"Yeah, thanks." He entered, shutting the door without turning his back to her. "Just wanted to chat a minute about that hotel lobby scene and the other changes Lori and I made. I know you were caught off guard. You're right. I…I promised to do a new location shot on the beach. However…"

"It's okay," Jewel stopped him, settling herself more deeply on a sofa piled with plump pillows in various shades of blue. She looked up at Taye. "Don't worry about it. You're the director. Lori is the head writer. You two certainly have the authority to change whatever you want." She crossed her legs, not missing the flicker of his eyes when her robe fell open and bared a good portion of her thigh.

"Well…I wanted to be sure you were okay with it," Taye remarked, sounding cautious and looking a bit uncomfortable.

"Forget about it. Everything is all right." Jewel pulled her shoulders back and adjusted her belt, but did not bother to cover her exposed leg. *Let him see what he wants so badly to touch,* she thought, suddenly wanting to annoy him as much as he'd annoyed her. "As a matter of fact," she continued, "I was just reading through the script and I think the changes definitely work. I like what you and Lori have done."

Now, Taye moved from the door over to Jewel and slid his index finger along the arm of the love seat. "Seriously? You like it?" he asked, piercing her heart with his electrifying brown eyes.

"Yes, I do."

"Good. Then you forgive me?" Taye asked, removing her script from the love seat to sit down beside her.

"Forgive you for what?" Jewel replied, aware that his thigh was braced against hers, that he'd filled all the empty space on the small sofa. "For leading me to believe that we'd have a location shoot on Catalina? For toning down Caprice's reaction to Darin? Or are you asking me to forgive you for kissing me last night after promising not to create an uneasy situation between us?"

"How about all three?" Taye suggested with a slow wink, inching even closer.

A burst of laughter. "I can't be *that* generous," Jewel flung back, trying to ease away from him, even though there was little room to maneuver.

"Why not grant all of my wishes?" he taunted. "What've you got to lose?"

Jewel caught her breath and held it tight when he placed his arm across the back of the love seat, dissolving all remaining space between them. He massaged her shoulder with his forefinger and thumb, then moved higher, lacing his fingers in her hair, stroking the nape of her neck.

"Whoa! Gimme a break," she said in an expulsion of breath. "I'm not Jeannie, just released from the bottle. I can grant you only one reprieve at a time," she tossed back, trying to kid along.

However, Taye didn't smile at her attempted joke. He rested his open palm on the back of her head and turned her toward him, gently touching his forehead to hers. Eyes downcast, he whispered. "If I can get only one reprieve, I guess I'll ask you to forgive me for altering the script, because I sure don't want to be forgiven for kissing you." He brushed the tip of her nose with his. "As a matter of fact, I'd like to do it again."

Jewel froze, unable—or unwilling—to back down.

Taye stamped her mouth with a solid kiss and then pulled back, letting his lips hover near hers until Jewel broke the slender thread of hesitation and surrendered.

Sliding flush against Taye, she accepted his challenge, kissing him with abandon, running her tongue over his, hungrily devouring his full warm lips with no thought of any restraint.

Well, here I am, right back where I was last night, she silently admonished, swallowing the small cry of pleasure rising in her throat. She melted under his touch, tightening her arms around his neck, feeling her body weighted against his and realizing that she was exactly where she wanted to be: swept away by Taye's self-assured yet tender pursuit. Capturing his lower lip between her teeth, she gently tugged, teased and savored the essence of their sensuous encounter. Her nipples hardened as he traced a line of kisses from her forehead to the corners of her eyes to the flushed hollows of her cheeks. When the urgent tap of his fingers begged her to unhook her bra, she complied, groaning in joy as his hands cupped her breasts and his thumbs brushed her nipples. With a moan, she draped a bare leg across his knees and scrunched even closer.

I need to stop. I've got to focus. In a minute. He has to go! Her warring thoughts fought a losing battle as she drifted deeper and deeper into the roaring rush of need that was cascading through her body.

With an easy shift, Taye pulled Jewel fully onto his lap. His firm erection nudged insistently into her flesh, throbbing for release. Tilting back her head, she accepted his wet kisses on the base of her throat, imagining what it would feel like to have him deep inside her, pumping, stroking and driving her completely over the edge.

Suddenly, through the foggy swirl of her fantasy seduction, Jewel heard two sharp taps on her dressing room door.

"Hey, Jewel, you ready for makeup?"

"Shana!" Jewel gasped, pushing back from Taye. "Ohmigod." She jumped off Taye's lap and stood, shaking out her hair, glaring down at him. She tightened the belt of her silk robe. "Whatever you were planning…no, no and no," she admonished, squaring her shoulders, wiping her lips with her fingers, shocked by how close she had come to surrendering to him right there in her dressing room!

"Shana! Yes, come in," Jewel called out, thankful for the interruption.

Quickly, Taye stood. He grabbed Jewel's copy of the script and held it over his prominent erection.

"We were clarifying a few script changes," he lamely offered as Shana entered.

Jewel moved over to her makeup table and sat down with her back to the mirror, facing Shana.

Taye promptly made for the door, but paused to cast Jewel a wicked grin over Shana's shoulder, wagging a finger at her.

Jewel gritted her teeth and rolled her eyes, urging him to go away.

"So, ready to get started?" Shana chatted, busily arranging her pots of lipstick, tubes of foundation and plastic containers of eye shadow and blush. "It's going to be a long day," she added, rubbing her brush into a pool of rose-colored powder.

"Tell me about it," Jewel replied, sagging in relief as soon as Taye disappeared. "Let's hope I can get through it without melting down completely."

Chapter 15

For two days, Jewel managed to keep her distance from Taye by arriving early at the studio, closeting herself in her dressing room until she had to be on the set and then leaving as soon as her work was done. With her car still in the shop, she was using a car service to transport her to and from the studio, making it easy to escape the temptation of either inviting Taye to her house or meeting him at his. As filming progressed, he was cordial, professional and cool, but friendly, treating Jewel exactly as any director ought to treat his star.

It was ten o'clock in the evening on Wednesday when Jewel walked onto *P & P Set One—Caprice Desmond's Bedroom.* As she entered the elegant cocoon of cream and white touched with splashes of gold, she stretched her neck and rolled her shoulders, releasing the tension of the longest, most intense day of shooting all week.

The entire cast had left the studio except for Jewel and Sonny, who had one final scene to finish. For the past hour, they had hammered their way through their dialogue with the practiced rhythm of two actors who had worked together so long that their seamless exchanges flowed in flawless ripples. Now, at the final block of their emotional exchange Jewel hesitated, unsure of how Taye wanted her placement in the bedroom scene.

"Taye," she called over to him. "I just don't feel this crossover to Darin's left as he's trying to maneuver me into bed. Does he touch me, guide me? What makes me want to follow him so easily after the blowout argument we just had?"

"Oh, that. Yeah, yeah. Let's see." Taye considered her query as he stepped onto the set. "Jewel, start toward me," he directed. "Now, Sonny, why don't you do this?" he suggested to the actor, demonstrating how he wanted Sonny to slip his arm around Jewel's waist, stopping her in midstride. "Then, you go like this," he continued, sweeping Jewel to his side as he guided her toward a four-poster bed draped in white gauze. He lifted the sheer canopy, led her beneath it and over to the foot of the bed.

Jewel's heart pounded as if she'd been chased across the set, not seductively maneuvered behind the filmy curtain that shielded them from view.

When Taye slanted his body at an angle over Jewel's, she saw a slight twitch of his upper lip. His lame attempt to smother a smile both infuriated and amused her. She didn't know whether to scold him or crush her mouth to his.

Taye firmed his hold on her arm, unnerving Jewel so much that she went weak. Damn! She actually *wanted* him to kiss her right there, on the set. How dangerous was that? After all her self-talk about not letting her emotions get in the way, she was itching to make love to him in Caprice Desmond's bed! Abruptly, Jewel snapped her arm free and moved away.

"Got it?" Taye asked, his tone warm, disarming.

With a languid blink of her eyes, she said, "Yes."

Taye returned to Sonny and told him, "That's a wrap for tonight."

"Good idea," Sonny agreed.

"Okay, everybody, that's it," Taye called out to the crew. "Time for everyone to go home."

Jewel wasted no time hurrying around the naked backboard of the set—thin walls thumbtacked with scribbled notes and timing charts. The familiar sounds of technicians and camera crew shutting down equipment and scattering from the studio came to her as she stepped over bundles of wire and snakelike tendrils of cables the size of her arm.

In her dressing room, Jewel stripped off her navy slacks, threw her blazer over a hanger, ripped her camisole over her head and yanked on her black silk robe. She uncapped a jar of cold cream and began to remove her makeup. However, she could not focus on the task. Setting the jar aside, she let her concerns float to surface, troubled by what had just happened. It had been a long time since she had felt such an emotional rush over any man and this dangerous flirting with Taye had to stop! What in the world had she been thinking? Had Sonny noticed anything? Had her response to Taye's embrace been evident to the camera crew? The technical director? She let out a worried sigh.

Her reactions to Taye were becoming disturbingly powerful and too real to ignore. How had she let this happen? She hadn't known the guy long enough to feel so strongly about him, yet she couldn't shake the feeling that her attraction to him was not simply a chemical reaction to a handsome, talented man. Something else was going on and she had better decide if she wanted to explore it further or shut it down. The choice was hers to make, not Taye's. If she became adamant about not getting involved with him, he would back off and leave her alone, wouldn't he?

Is that what I want? She groaned in confusion. *Oh God, I don't know.* But one thing was certain: she did not want her heart to remain as empty as a darkened stage. She wanted Taye Elliott to step in, shine the spotlight on her desire and initiate a wonderful love affair.

Sounds beautiful, but what's the downside? she silently probed, setting her emotions aside to take a practical approach. *Heartbreak, humiliation, embarrassment, possible damage to my career. The same mess that happened after Chandler Jeffries dumped me.*

Jewel jammed two fingers into the jar of cold cream and slathered the white makeup remover across her forehead. *Okay, been there, done that. Seen that movie. So, what's the upside?* she continued, grabbing a tissue, cleansing her skin with fast swipes. *The erotic sensation of sinking totally into Taye Elliott's world. Of touching his soul and allowing him to touch mine. The absolute joy of making love to the man I so desperately crave. Of ending these stupid self-imposed restrictions and not losing out on love.*

The gentle tap-tap at her door broke her concentration. Jewel frowned. The knock sounded too damn familiar and the fact that she now recognized Taye's bid for entry into her dressing room—and that it sent her heart into a spin—was ridiculous!

Without asking who it was, she finished wiping off her makeup and flung open the door. Taye stepped in, closed it and then simply stood and watched her. Jewel glared at her visitor, not sure where to start, her careful analysis of the situation suddenly evaporating.

What should I do? Play a role or play it out for real? However, she didn't have time to speak and didn't resist when she saw the flicker of desire in his eyes or felt his grip on her upper arms as he swept her flush against his chest.

"Everyone's gone," he murmured.

"Why did you come here?" she groaned against his shirt, knowing she had lost her battle of wills.

"Thought you might need a little more coaching." His reply was savagely raw and clear in intent. His hands slipped down and cupped her elbows in gentle, possessive restraint.

"Coaching? Um, that's not necessary. I know exactly what I'm doing," she muttered, her insides roiling with a curious pull that tugged at her heart and struck a vibrant chord of need. She tried to turn away, but he caught her by the hand and guided her toward the sofa where she slumped down, having lost all control.

"Mmm-hmm. Are you sure you know what you're doing?" He knelt on the floor, his face level with hers.

"As sure as I want to be right now," she admitted, not resisting when he swept her robe off her shoulders and tossed it aside. He sat back on his heels, watching, not touching her, as if waiting for her to tell him what she wanted.

Jewel challenged Taye with eyes that struggled to see beyond this electrifying connection, wanting to be sure.

He's giving me a way out, she realized, torn by the intensity of the moment. Impulsively, she reached out to him and drew him close, not moving when he slid his hands over the flat of her stomach and tested the rise of her hips. Her eyes fluttered closed. She had made up her mind. She wanted him and didn't give a damn if having Taye Elliott was a big mistake.

Eyes shut, Jewel sank into darkness, where she sensed his movements as he took off his shirt. Did she dare open her eyes to look at him? Dare try to stop what she wanted to happen? Would words even come out if she tried to speak?

When Taye's naked chest made contact with her bare breasts, Jewel pressed her mouth into the curve of his neck and smothered an eruption of joy. Clinging to him, she let the heat of his skin melt her apprehensions, felt the weight of his hands as they massaged the length of her back, heard the sound of his voice as he murmured all the right nothings, resounding like music in her soul.

"I know you're a pro," he whispered. "But I think your director can show you a few things." He teasingly touched the bones in her spine while placing a line of kisses across the ridge of her shoulders and then inch by inch, raw second by raw second, he moved his mouth lower and lower until he captured a hard nipple and circled it with his tongue.

Head thrown back, Jewel squinted down at Taye, considering her comeback to that remark, aware that her response would set the stage for the next act of this dangerous liaison, but she was ready to perform. "I never said I knew *everything,*" she countered in a silky tone. "And isn't it your job, as director, to call the shots?"

"Correct," he softly replied, not letting go of her swollen nipple.

"All right then," she drawled, stringing out her words. "You may call the shots, but don't forget…I'm the one who'll interpret your instructions."

"I'm sure you'll never let me forget it," he admitted, nuzzling the warm spot between her breasts before easing down to taste her belly button, inching even lower to send his tongue probing into the triangle of thick brown hair covering the most tender spot on her body.

A lick, a flutter, a deliciously intense tug. Jewel arched forward, relaxed and then opened herself wide enough to give Taye space to pleasure her in whatever manner he wanted. She shifted upward under his hands, which had recaptured both of her breasts, his fingers rhythmically rotating her nipples in precise tandem with the motion of his tongue. As he delighted in pleasuring her pulsing core, she luxuriated in the magical, musical cadence he was creating in her body—a silent song that rose in a crescendo of heat and desire to climax in a dangerous but thrilling explosion—which crashed Jewel back to earth when the dressing room telephone rang.

"Don't answer," Taye groaned, lifting his head, squinting one eye at her.

"I have to. If I don't, security might come knocking." Untangling herself from Taye's lock on her body, she leaned over and grabbed the receiver.

"Oh, yes. Thanks. I'll be out in five minutes," she spoke into the phone.

Taye sat up, giving her an annoyed look.

"My car is outside waiting," she told Taye.

"Cancel it. I'll drive you home."

"Oh, no, you're not," she protested, hurrying to get up. She grabbed her jeans, pulled them on and then started on her blouse. "I really can't trust myself to allow you near my house right now. You know, Taye." She stopped buttoning her shirt to level a stern look at him. "It's really a good thing the phone rang, you know?"

"No, it wasn't. Let me take you home, Jewel, so we can…"

She rolled her eyes at him. "Pick up where we left off?" she finished, giving him a mischievous grin.

"Yeah. Exactly." He did not deny.

"No way," she tossed back in a lighter tone. "Getting out of here now is what I need to do." She grabbed her purse.

He shot her a look of exasperation.

Jewel huffed her annoyance, a hand at her hip. "Taye, please! We were saved by the bell…or by the phone, at least. Fooling around at the studio is stupid! This absolutely cannot happen again! Never!" She opened the door, but turned around to tell him, "We'd better continue to keep our distance okay? So do not come knocking on my dressing room door again." She pressed two fingers to her mouth, gathering her composure, certain she was doing the right thing. "Oh, and lock up when you leave, all right?"

Taye scowled at her, clearly annoyed.

"Don't look at me like that. You know we can't do this." A beat. "See you tomorrow," Jewel told him and then she was gone.

Chapter 16

The next two days on the set of *The Proud and the Passion-ate* went smoothly, even though they lasted long into the evening. Taye kept everyone on schedule, accomplished what he set out to do and felt positive about the pace of the work. The cast accepted him, the crew was cooperative and so far, he hadn't received any negative feedback from the studio.

However, he was worried about Jewel. She had begun to play Caprice Desmond with cool familiarity instead of the brash crispness he wanted. She was prepared every day, knew her lines and executed them with precision, but she was not deliv-ering the spark he'd seen in her earlier performances.

Taye tapped his desk with his pen, thinking—hoping he was not the cause of this clampdown of her emotions. *No, she's just overworked,* he rationalized.

Daytime television moved at an incredible pace, with the actors working extremely hard, for very long hours. Jewel often memorized as many as thirty-five pages of dialogue a day and usually got one take to get it right. The network produced two-hundred fifty shows a year, and the grueling schedule could take its toll. Taye understood that Jewel was focused on her work and driven to succeed, but how long could she continue in this intensely fast-paced environment without losing some of her stamina and grit? He just hoped she wasn't holding back because of him.

Since their encounter in her dressing room, Taye had kept his promise to treat her with professional respect. He didn't visit her dressing room, didn't offer her rides home and even though tempted to, didn't call her at home in the evening. He was determined not to upset her or infer that he expected anything from her except her best work.

At the studio, he was the competent, all-about-work director she expected him to be. However, if Jewel could see what was going on inside his head, he was sure she'd find a tangled mess of unfulfilled longing and fantasy dreams about a love affair with her.

Now, Taye swiveled to his computer, clicked on the browser at the top of his screen and surfed over to Jewel's Web site, which he'd begun to visit quite often. He loved the photo that dominated her home page. Her sexy red dress accentuated her curves. Her alluring smile zapped him with a jolt of desire. Her hair, tumbling in loose curls around her face, created a seductive, taunting vision and her luminous brown eyes cut straight into his heart.

Oh, what I'd love to do to this woman! Taye thought, swiveling back and forth in nervous longing as he clicked on the tab for *Jewel's Favorite Things.* He had almost memorized the daytime diva's favorite foods, wines, vacation spots, movies, books and restaurants. He was pleased to see that Tansu House on Rodeo Drive was one of her favorite restaurants. He'd visited the posh eatery a few times after his split from Rona, when he'd felt like blowing a bundle of cash on a fancy date, which hadn't happened very often. In fact, now that he thought about it, he had had exactly four real dates in the last twenty-two months, all with different women, all disappointing, all just to pass the time.

Taye had never been a true "dating" kind of man, so maybe that was why he'd married so impulsively. He had never wanted a series of lovers parading in and out of his life, taking what they wanted and moving on. He'd always imagined that he would settle down with one special woman, one person to love him, whom he could love back. Was that what he saw in Jewel? Was that why she was lodged in his head like a magnet stuck to metal? Why couldn't he stop thinking about her, wanting to love her, yearning for a deeper understanding of what would make her happy?

Frustrated, Taye clicked off the computer monitor and slipped a disk into his DVD player to review the dailies, which he'd already seen three times. After watching yesterday's work once more, he felt satisfied but not thrilled.

Anything less than fantastic is not gonna cut it with the network, he worried. Something was off and he knew what it was.

"Hey, Taye, got a minute?" Sonny Burton asked, pausing in the open door to interrupt Taye's mental musings.

"Yeah, sure," Taye replied, jerking his head to motion Sonny in.

After slipping into the chair on the other side of Taye's desk, Sonny leaned forward, his hands dangling between his long legs. He was dressed in a green-and-white jogging outfit and had a towel around his neck, obviously having just finished his workout in the studio gym.

"I didn't know you were in the building," Taye said, recalling that both Sonny and Jewel were not scheduled today. "Just can't stay away even on your Friday off?"

Sonny grinned and shook his head. "It's not love for *P & P* that's got me here, I assure you. Just wanted to get in a good workout today because tomorrow…is my wife's family reunion picnic at Topanga Beach. And, well, let's just say I plan to partake of every dish on the table. Lyn's mom, her five sisters and all of her aunts are famous for their cooking and I plan to enjoy myself."

Taye chuckled in agreement. "Well, man, you've got my permission to indulge. The weather oughta be perfect, so you'll have a great day at the beach." He scooted his chair closer to his desk and picked up a pen, which he tapped on the blotter. "So, what's on your mind?"

A shrug, a quick blink of his eyes and a tilt of his chin before Sonny answered. "Well…I been wondering. Is anything wrong with Jewel?" He licked his lips and frowned. "She's seemed off her mark all week. Kinda cool to me, you know? I was wondering if you knew something I didn't. Is she upset with me? I know she's had that problem with her car, but it seems like she's not connecting. I'm just not feelin' the same kind of vibes we used to have, you know?"

Sonny's assessment of Jewel's behavior went straight to Taye's gut, settling there in an uncomfortable lump. So, Sonny sensed it, too.

"She's had a lot to adjust to. I think she's not quite over Brad's death," Taye offered. "They were very close, weren't they?"

"Sure. We all loved and respected Brad, but I don't think that's it. She doesn't seem sad…just uptight. As if all she wants to do is get through the scene and back into her dressing room. That is *not* the Jewel I know. She's always been the last one to leave the set, the one who sticks around to make sure the newest member of the cast feels included. Kinda like the mother hen of our group. Now, she comes and goes like nothing matters except getting through her lines and getting out of here."

"Well, Sonny, you certainly know Jewel better than I do." *But God how I want to know her better.* "If you're sensing something is off balance with her, I believe you." *She's got me so off balance that I no longer know what stable ground feels like anymore.* "Want me to talk to her?" *And say what? Cut out the cool-acting crap and turn on the passion? Get rid of your artificial barriers and let me make love to you?*

"Would you talk to her?" Sonny asked, looking relieved. "You know I can't. It's not my place, but I wanted to let you know that I'm concerned. I wouldn't have brought all this up if I didn't love Jewel like a sister and worry about her. She's a true pro. She's got it all going on. So, I just don't understand why she's holding back like this. If it's me, let me know, Taye, and I'll do whatever I can to make her feel more comfortable."

"I doubt it's about you, Sonny. We all have a lot riding on this season and there's a great deal of pressure on everyone. Tension's running high right now. It can create a real strain."

"Maybe she just needs to relax," Sonny guessed. "I keep telling her she works too damn hard and needs to take time out to just play around. I invited her to join me and Lyn at Topanga for the picnic, but she said she'd be busy with some charity she's involved with. Taye, maybe you can get her to lighten up and find the groove she needs to turn up the heat."

"I don't know about that, but I'll try 'cause we've got to pull out the stops, wrap up this story line and get a bump in the ratings."

"I heard that," Sonny agreed. "I'll bet the suits in the head office have you under the microscope."

"For sure and I plan to give them what they want. A damn great show every day." Taye tried to laugh off his assessment, even though he knew it was a fact. His ass was on the line and he had better produce.

Sonny stood, raised his hand in a salute of appreciation and said, "Thanks, Taye. You won't say anything to Jewel about my talkin' to you, will you?"

"Of course not, Sonny. This conversation stays between us."

After Sonny left, Taye stared glumly at the empty chair, feeling his frustration grow. He was being too careful with Jewel and she was coming off as rote, uninspired and detached. Was their wary avoidance of each other affecting the way he directed her, the way she came across on the screen? Obviously, Sonny saw what Taye hadn't wanted to admit and now he had to fix it. Fast. But how could Taye move Jewel onto stable ground where they both could find their footing?

Relax, Sonny had advised. *Make Jewel get out and enjoy herself.*

A sly grin slid over Taye's face as he grabbed his BlackBerry and began to text, certain he had just the cure for the tension that had both him and Jewel on edge.

Chapter 17

"Need anything else before I go?" Carmie inquired, poking her head into the den where Jewel was talking with Chuck Davies, her Statewide Insurance agent.

Jewel glanced at her assistant, who was juggling a pile of clothing destined for the dry cleaners while digging into her patchwork leather purse for her car keys. "No, nothing, thanks. Coffee's fine," Jewel told Carmie. "Better get going before traffic builds up."

"I'm gone," Carmie replied, jangling her keys. "The dry cleaners. Royal Street Market. The post office. Nothing else?"

"That's about it," Jewel agreed.

"Be back in about an hour."

"Take your time," Jewel advised, waving at Carmie and hoping that Davies would not take up too much of her Friday morning. She handed him a cup of coffee, settled back in her chair and told him, once again, the details of her accident.

"How fast were you going?" he asked, tilting forward, as if to hear her better.

"Twenty, maybe twenty-five. The speed limit. I'm sure because I glanced at the speedometer when I turned the corner."

"Did you try to stop?"

"Of course I did, but there wasn't time. All of a sudden the van was in front of me."

"Had it stalled?"

"I don't know! When I realized it wasn't moving, it was too late." Jewel knew it was Davies's job to get as much information from her as possible, but his pointed questions were beginning to annoy her. "I was entirely at fault. I wasn't paying attention," she confessed, her mind drifting back to the day of the crash.

Taye Elliott was on my mind, she silently mused. *My head was full of him! That's why I wasn't paying attention. I should blame him for wrecking my car, for getting me into this stupid situation.*

"And you're sure the van wasn't damaged?" Davies probed, snapping Jewel out of her mental wandering.

Quickly, she refocused on the agent. "That's right. But what about *my* car?" she pressed "It's been a week and it's still in the shop. Is Statewide going to cover the repairs or not?"

Davies let a short silence build between them, as if deciding how to answer. Finally, he gave Jewel a slow nod and a blink of his pale blue eyes. "Oh, yes. Your insurance covers all repairs to your car, but that's not the problem." He spread out a fan of papers on the table, taking care to arrange each one equidistant from the next.

Here it comes, Jewel thought, steeling herself for some paperwork nightmare that would require hours and hours of her time and attention. "Then what *is* the problem, Mr. Davies?"

"Your accident is a bit more complicated than you assumed, Miss Blaine," he started as he lightly touched each of the papers. "Mr. Weng, the driver of the van, and each of his three brothers…the passengers in the van…have filed claims for…"

Jewel snapped alert and stopped him in midsentence. "Filed claims? Why? How?"

"You gave Mr. Weng an insurance card, didn't you?"

"Well, yes. But he drove off before we could even talk about insurance. What kind of claims did they file?"

Davies picked up one of the multipage documents and began to read. "They want compensation for soft-tissue injury, mental distress and whiplash, including payment of all medical bills related to their diagnoses."

"No way!" Jewel almost laughed. "This is impossible! It has to be some kind of a scam! Mr. Weng was not hurt and his brothers seemed all right when they approached me. Why all of a sudden, they're hurt? They were fine when they drove off!"

"Were there any witnesses?"

Jewel's mind whirled back. She recalled how relieved she'd felt that no one had been paying attention to what was going on. Now, she wished an army of folks had run over to gawk at her, that the paparazzi had descended and snapped photos to back up her story.

"No! I don't know! Maybe there were witnesses," she admitted to Davies. "But I'm telling you the truth. It was *not* the kind of accident that could have caused physical injury. As soon as I mentioned calling an ambulance, the driver took off."

"That's not the way Mr. Weng says it happened. He claims that he and his brothers were in serious pain when they got out of the van and that they begged you to help them. They left the scene and drove themselves to the hospital because you refused to call an ambulance."

"Hell no! Not true!"

"Well, if the medical records back up their claims of injury, we may have to make a significant offer to settle this." Davies paused and gave up a small, tight cough. "That could mean an increase in your Statewide premiums, Miss Blaine."

"You can't be for real!" Now, Jewel was enraged. The idea of settling with the Wengs and facing higher insurance premiums was incredible. "Isn't there anything you can do?"

"I have no reason to doubt that you're telling the truth and I understand your outrage," Davies said. "However, you may have become the victim of a pretty routine insurance scam."

"Really?"

"Yes, as much as I hate to admit it, scams like these are fairly common. Statewide will get the medical records and if they support the claim, we'll settle fairly with the Wengs. However, soft-tissue damage is difficult to disprove."

Jewel drew in a deep breath to steady herself, mad as hell. "So, they get paid for faking injuries and I foot the bill with higher insurance premiums? What's fair about that?"

"Your premiums may *not* go up. All depends on how large of a settlement we have to pay. This may take time to sort out, but we'll get to the bottom of it before any checks are issued."

In a calmer voice, Jewel stated what she knew was behind this outrageous development. "Mr. Davies, this is happening to me because the Wengs did some checking and found out I'm on television. Right?"

"Could be."

"So, they think Statewide will cut huge checks to quietly settle this, that I won't make a fuss?"

"Probably."

Davies's reply made Jewel even angrier. She thought about Diana Ross, Brandi, Halle Berry—celebrities whose automobile accidents and ensuing court cases had made headlines, creating media distractions that carried negative repercussions and which had ended in multimillion-dollar settlements. With *P & P* fighting for ratings, a new director on board and her career on the line, the last thing Jewel needed was for the public to think that she was a negligent driver who was balking at paying for injuries she'd inflicted. What a no-win situation!

"So," Davies said, putting his papers back into his briefcase. "I'll be in touch with you as the claim progresses and we'll get your car fixed as soon as possible. Thanks for taking the time to meet with me, Miss Blaine. And don't worry. Leave everything to us."

"I will," Jewel replied, thinking, *What choice do I have? I was at fault, so I guess I'll have to suffer the consequences.*

* * *

As soon as Carmie returned from running her errands, Jewel filled her in on the bad news.

"Hmm, hmm," Carmie murmured over her shoulder while putting the fresh vegetables she'd purchased at Royal Market into the refrigerator. "I had a bad feeling about that accident as soon as you told me the men drove off. Now, you see why you need a driver?"

"Come on, Carmie," Jewel urged. "Give that a rest. What I need is proof. I wish I could find someone who could verify what really happened." Jewel came up behind Carmie and placed a hand on her shoulder. "Will you drive me to the corner of Windsor and Eighth?"

"Now?" Carmie whirled around, looking skeptical. "Uh-uh. No way. Leave it to Statewide to investigate. You don't need to play detective."

"Yes, I do. Come on," Jewel decided, grabbing Carmie's car keys off the counter and directing her assistant out the back door.

"Okay, okay," Carmie reluctantly agreed, climbing into her shiny red Chevy Blazer SUV. "Get in. Guess we're going back to the scene of the crime."

However, once they were on their way, Carmie seemed to warm to the adventure, telling Jewel, "Somebody had to see something. In a city like Los Angeles, there's always someone watching someone else. We've just got to find out who it was on that particular day."

"Exactly," Jewel concurred. "Even though no one stopped or came over to see what was happening, there has to be a witness."

Jewel's nerves were strung so tightly she wanted to scream, but instead of dwelling on her frustration, she forced herself to calm down. Reaching for the button to turn on the radio, she glanced at Carmie. "Mind if I listen to Jazz Café?"

"Not at all. Put it on whatever you want."

As soft jazz filled the car, Jewel tried to focus on the music, but her mind kept returning to the questions she wished she'd asked Mr. Davies. Did she need an attorney? Had anyone checked Weng's driving record? His criminal record? Maybe he was a serial scammer who had done this kind of thing before.

When her BlackBerry buzzed, she dismissed her worry and accessed a text message from Taye:

Are you free Saturday? Want to check possible location site.

Go location scouting with Taye? She paused and then typed:

Where? When? Who else is going?

Just outside L.A. About five o'clock. Fred, if he can get away.

Certainly, she had nothing pressing to do, although she'd begged off going to Sonny's family reunion with a half-truth about a commitment. What fun would there be for her at Sonny's lively family gathering, where she would only be an outsider looking in?

Maybe she ought to go. Besides, Fred would appreciate her cooperating with Taye. All week, she'd gone out of her way to keep things calm on the set and it had worked. She'd followed Taye's direction without questioning his interpretation of a scene or disagreeing on anything. Whenever Taye stepped forward to demonstrate how he wanted Jewel to position herself, she'd treated him with cool detachment, as if he were no more important than a plumber who'd come to fix a leak. She'd gone through each scene with perfect-pitch timing, never missing a cue or dropping a line. Outwardly, she trusted him with her emotions, even though a warm jolt of desire still shot through her whenever he got too near.

Jewel studied her BlackBerry screen, feeling the sexual draw that flared inside her, simmering, growing, draining her resolve. How long could this continue? Sooner or later one of them would be forced to act. Setting aside her unwanted reaction, she texted: Okay. Where do we meet?

Will send car 4 you at 5.

OK.

Jewel shut down her BlackBerry, pleased with her decision to treat this invitation in a rational, professional manner. *I've been too self-absorbed. I've got to let go of this obsessive worry and focus on keeping my balance with Taye. Nothing disruptive could possibly happen on a routine location scout.*

After arriving at the intersection of Windsor and Eighth, Carmie parked in front of the convenience store on the corner. Jewel went inside and conducted a one-sided mishmash of an interview with the Middle Eastern man working there, only to learn that he'd seen nothing on the day in question and was sorry he couldn't be more helpful.

As she made her way up and down the street, Jewel received similar responses: no one knew anything and no one wanted to get involved. Realizing there was little to accomplish with this approach, Jewel asked Carmie to drive her home.

Hunched over the steering wheel, eyes nearly level with the rim, Carmie offered some advice. "You could put up a billboard or place a notice in the neighborhood paper announcing a reward. That'd get somebody's attention." Carmie was clearly trying to put a positive spin on their disappointing mission.

"No, not a good idea," Jewel threw back with alarm. "I'd get a bunch of crank calls and all kinds of crazies would come up with a lot of misinformation that wouldn't do anything but complicate matters. Anyway, the press would jump on it…causing a ton of bad publicity."

Carmie murmured something under her breath, seeming unconvinced as she scooted even closer to the steering wheel and squinted through her spiral curly bangs. "Don't be so fast to say what you *won't* do," she cautioned rather sternly. "This situation might be easier to resolve than you think. Don't get so caught up in protecting yourself that you get stuck."

Jewel let Carmie's words sink in, realizing how valid they might be. To solve this, she might have to move off safe ground and take a few risks. She might have to change her approach to get the results she wanted.

Even with Taye Elliott, she thought, recalling their brief encounter in her dressing room. His mouth between her legs, his fingers rotating her nipples, his lemon-fresh scent filling her head. He was a challenge, all right. Perhaps if she stopped allowing him to test her and if she removed the barriers she'd so staunchly built around her heart, she might be able to solve her Taye Elliott problem. *I might even discover that there's nothing to worry about, that the chemistry between us is just an illusion. Only one way to find out,* she decided, tucking Carmie's advice into a corner of her mind.

Chapter 18

Jewel sipped champagne from a cool crystal flute as the stretch limousine maneuvered onto the Golden State Freeway. *An hour's ride,* the driver had told her when he'd picked her up at her house and helped her into the luxurious car that had every possible amenity: satellite TV, a fully stocked bar, a selection of music at the touch of a finger. It also had a fax machine, a laptop computer and a private phone with numbers for airlines, hotels and the best restaurants in L.A. already programmed into its call log. The limo was spacious and empty except for her, making her feel very small but nonetheless important. Taye really knew how to treat his cast and she appreciated his providing such comfortable transportation. Brad Fortune had never done anything like this.

Where is this mysterious place and what story line is in the works? Jewel wondered, trying to guess why Taye wanted to keep it a secret. Maybe he thought a change of setting would add a touch of intrigue to the show, pump up viewers' curiosity, grab a few more shares in the ratings war. He had certainly been vague when he'd texted Jewel a second time and told her to wear comfortable walking shoes and very casual clothing as they would be outside most of the time. She hoped her dark tan khakis, white cotton sweater set and ankle-high boots were appropriate for wherever he had in mind.

When her BlackBerry buzzed, she saw it was Marlena and answered right away, eager to pass some time. When Jewel told Marlena that she was in a limo and did not know her destination, Marlena jumped to a surprising conclusion.

"A limo? Champagne? A mystery destination? Sounds more like you're going on a fantasy date than a location shoot to me," she proposed.

"You need to quit. This is strictly business," Jewel countered.

"Who are you trying to fool? Hello? I've met Taye Elliott, remember? I know how those sexy bedroom eyes of his can beg for attention and how easy it would be for you to fall under his spell. Be careful, Jewel. You've gotta work with this fine brother every day. Don't get mixed up in anything personal."

"I am not *even* tempted to go there."

"So you say…. Think I don't know how starved you are for the attention of a *real* man?" A beat. "On-screen lovers don't count, you know?"

"Marlena. I'm *not* starving for attention from any man and even if I did decide to spend some of the little free time I have with Taye Elliott, so what? He's nice. He's respectful and he's divorced," Jewel countered sharply.

"But he's still your director," Marlena shot back.

"I know that! And I have no intention of crossing any lines. I know what you're so worried about," Jewel said, recalling the pain of those isolated, lonely months following her public disgrace after the Chandler Jeffries affair.

"Exactly. You certainly don't need to get involved with Taye Elliott. Still, you do need to get your personal life together. Why does a beautiful, smart, successful sister like you want to act as if you don't miss having a *real* family? A husband. Kids. Pushy in-laws. The kinds of relatives you *have* to love, but who can drive you a little bit crazy."

"Oh? Like yours, I guess?" Jewel teased.

"Precisely," Marlena agreed with a short laugh. "Although I wouldn't wish my distracted CrackBerry husband and two spoiled teenage daughters or picky in-laws on anyone. They test my last nerve every day, but I still love 'em to death."

"Your husband is a dear. Rhonda and Tonya are gorgeous, smart girls. They deserve to be spoiled. And Gerry's parents are adorable. Picky, but still adorable. You shouldn't complain so much."

"Oh, it's just a bad habit of mine.... Anyway, no one at my house takes me seriously. But I am serious about you. You don't want to be alone forever, do you? Who's gonna take care of you when you're old, fat and gray?"

"First of all, that is not going to happen. Second, I'm happy with my life as it is. What kind of shape do you think my career would be in if I had a husband and kids to deal with? Long ago, I realized that acting is all I need and I've managed to get this far by not second-guessing my decision to remain single and unattached."

"How you can settle for make-believe romance on a soap opera instead of the *real* thing escapes me. I've been married for thirteen years and I'm still in love with my honey. More than ever."

"And I'm happy for you," Jewel replied. "But I'm different. Life is perfect as it is, so stop worrying about my getting involved with Taye Elliott or anyone else, okay?"

"All right, all right. Guess I'm way off base," Marlena conceded.

"Absolutely. Anyway, Taye and I already had that discussion. We pledged to be strictly artistic colleagues. Nothing personal is ever going to happen."

"So, that means you two have already touched on subjects of the heart, huh?"

"I wouldn't say he touched my heart, but he did...well, he touched my lips," Jewel teased.

"I knew it!"

"With his finger," Jewel clarified, not daring to disclose any more.

"Jewel! You are *so* bad! When did this go down?"

"After a strictly business meeting. At my house." Jewel could not resist throwing that in, just to get a reaction from Marlena.

"Oh my God. He's been to your house? Tell me you two didn't wind up…"

"No! We didn't! You are terrible!" Jewel flung out, stopping Marlena in her tracks. "His finger-kiss was simply his way of sealing our truce not to make each other uncomfortable at the studio, so don't read anything else into it."

"Okay, okay. I'm simply calling it as I feel it." Marlena backed off. "I've been praying for you to remain focused on what's important, so you'll be strong enough to get out of the way of anything or anyone that might hurt you or your career."

"And I appreciate that, but I can assure you I am not in danger of running off course. I'll make sure your prayers are not in vain."

"Thank you," Marlena muttered with a sigh.

"Gotta go."

"Call me when you get back in town," Marlena said. "And I want details, you hear?"

"Sure, Marlena," Jewel replied with a shake of her head.

Shutting off her phone, she sat back and looked out the window, feeling adventurous and excited about this mysterious destination.

Location shoots could be entertaining, even glamorous, but they could also be mundane, boring and even dangerous, depending on what the story line required. During Jewel's run with *P & P,* Caprice Desmond had been proposed to on top of a fifty-story building in Manhattan, serenaded by mariachis atop a pyramid in Mexico, tossed overboard from a sailboat in the Bahamas and publicly trashed by a reporter at a fashion show in Paris. And always, Caprice had landed on her feet.

And then, there was the shoot on Galveston Island, which had ended so tragically with Brad's untimely death. It seemed so long ago, when in fact it had been only a month—a month in which a hell of a lot had happened.

Shaking off sad memories, Jewel reached for the golden box of Godiva chocolates and opened it. After deciding on a nut cluster caramel, she sank deeper into the limo's leather cushions and watched as L.A. traffic thinned out and the rugged California countryside began to slide past her darkened window.

Taye pulled his truck up to the locked gate that spanned the deserted gravel drive and scrutinized the black wrought-iron fence securing entry to his ranch. Large black metal letters spelled out the name: Double Pass. He had chosen that name because it represented his stunt work days, when he'd doubled for celebrities who'd been more than willing to stand on the sidelines to let Taye Elliott pass for them. Those had been glorious, adventurous times, but they were long gone, as his beloved ranch would soon be, too.

Taye slammed the door of his Hummer shut with a crack and stalked over to the large blue-and-white For Sale sign hanging on the front gate. How awful it looked, hanging there, beckoning strangers to inspect the place that had been his most private retreat. With a rip, Taye tore down the sign and tossed it to the side of the road, where it landed beneath a thick stand of brush. The prospect of anyone other than himself owning Double Pass made him sick to his stomach and for now, he wanted to forget that it was on the market and enjoy the solitude of the peaceful countryside as if nothing would ever change.

In fact, he was beginning to think that no one was interested in his paradise in the country, as there had been no serious offers since he'd put the ranch up for sale. Rona was complaining that the asking price was too high, but Taye had shot her down. Community property or not, he refused to bend to Rona's demands that he reduce the price. He was not about to give his ranch away just so she could get her hands on half of the money. He'd fight that to the end, so until Double Pass sold, it was still his and he planned to enjoy it.

Taye pushed back his well-worn, tan felt cowboy hat, hooked his thumbs into the belt loops of his jeans and squinted at the gray-green mountains in the distance—tall, towering and protective of the piece of heaven he'd managed to carve out of the land. His ranch was not as fancy as many in the area, but it was exactly what he wanted. Four hundred acres of undeveloped scrub with a modest ranch house, a stable for his horses and a shady patio with a swimming pool where he could be alone and relax.

The one-story house at the base of the mountains blended naturally into the landscape. A fully modern lodge with rustic, western-chic furnishings inside and desert-themed landscaping around the house. It had a red tile roof, a rough-hewn timber facade and a shady front porch rimmed with knotty pine logs.

Beyond the lodge, closer to the mountain base was the barn and next to it, a stable where Taye kept two horses named Strike and Player. Next to those buildings was a neat four-room cabin where Whit Zane, his groundskeeper, resided.

Whit was as tough and sinewy as the maverick cowboys he'd played as a young man in films in the fifties and the sixties. He was one of the few black actors who'd been lucky enough to get parts in westerns during that time. Whit had worked with legends like Clint Eastwood and Burt Reynolds, playing the intuitive member of a posse or the deputy sheriff of a small western town. After aging out of acting and falling on hard times, he'd been thrilled to accept Taye's offer of lodging and meals to watch over Double Pass.

Now, Taye got back into his Hummer and headed up the driveway toward the house, his mind clicking through everything he'd asked Whit to arrange before making himself scarce for the weekend. Stock the kitchen with ready-to-grill chicken, shrimp and steaks; put his favorite wine and champagne in the fridge to cool; make sure the pool was clean and the patio was spotless; and place fresh flowers all around the house.

After parking under the car port on the sunny side of the house, Taye went around back to the patio. The early-evening sunlight cast a muted sheen of yellow on the white flagstone floor and blushed the rattan furniture's multicolor cushions into a rich floral blend. A three-tier fountain of huge clay pots spilled a tinkling stream of water into a low basin filled with flowers. A few feet off the patio, a grotto-lush pool was surrounded by a thick tangle of bamboo, hibiscus, ferns and pampas grass, creating a curtain of privacy to shut out the world. The patio and pool area was one of Taye's favorite spots to sit and read scripts, work on his laptop, nap in total privacy or simply do nothing but float on his back in the aqua-blue water and dream.

And I have to give up all of this to get Rona out of my life, he silently complained. But as disconcerting as that was, Taye was willing to go that route if it meant he would be free. Free to be with the woman he truly loved, the one he now knew was meant to be his partner in life.

The sound of car tires crunching on the gravel road yanked Taye out of his thoughts. He circled to the front of the house, shaded his eyes with one hand and peered down the driveway at the white limousine that was approaching. When the sleek car pulled to a stop in the circular drive at his front door, Taye hurried over, just as the driver got out and opened the door for Jewel, who stepped out and looked around.

"You made it!" Taye beamed at her, hurrying closer. He held out his hand, which she clasped with hers.

"Yes. Here I am," Jewel replied, letting go of his hand to turn full circle as she surveyed her surroundings. "Beautiful! Absolutely gorgeous."

"Go look around. I'll catch up," Taye told her, turning his attention to the driver.

Jewel started across the lawn toward a yellow rosebush that was covered with early blooms. She bent down, smelled a flower and then looked back at Taye. "This is wonderful country," she called out. "But exactly where am I?" She pointed down the driveway toward the tall entry gate. "Double Pass? Someone's ranch, I'm guessing?"

"I'll explain everything later," he yelled over to Jewel,

turning back to the chauffeur. "No problem finding the place?" he asked, accepting the invoice the man gave to him.

"None," the driver responded as he tore off a receipt and handed it to Taye. "GPS makes it easy, bro."

"Good." Taye chuckled, adding a generous tip to the charge slip and signing his name in a quick scribble.

"Need a pickup later?" the driver asked.

"I…I don't know. Uh, I'll call you if I do," Taye said, stuffing his receipt into the pocket of his jeans.

"You got my number," the chauffer replied. He got back into the limo, waved to Taye and then swept down the circular drive and onto the road.

"So, did you enjoy your Friday off?" Taye said to Jewel, joining her.

She groaned and mocked a scowl. "You won't believe what happened with my car…the insurance company. It's a real mess."

"Yeah? What's wrong?" he asked, giving her a puzzled look.

As they walked back toward the house, Jewel filled Taye in on her meeting with Chuck Davies, the Wengs' unfair claim and her failed attempt to find a witness to support her version of the accident.

"Sounds like it could get nasty," Taye said, stopping at the foot of the porch steps to focus on Jewel. "I'd get a lawyer's advice, if I were you."

"You know, I was thinking the same thing. CBC's got a legal expert on retainer who's very sharp. I got to know her pretty well when *P & P* had a story line involving a murder-by-poisoning case. She impressed me as the kind of lawyer who can dig the truth out of any situation."

"Good. Call her," Taye advised, uncomfortable with what he'd just heard. Jewel didn't need that kind of pressure right now. He'd invited her out to the country so she could unwind and relax, to hopefully make it easier for her to let down her guard with him on the set. But Taye had to admit that he also wanted to find out what, if anything, was really developing between them. Sure, he'd promised Sonny that he'd discuss

Jewel's change of attitude toward her costar, but Taye had no intention of upsetting her by bringing up that subject. *Everything will fall into line at work once we stop zigzagging around each other. Either we have something worth pursuing or we don't and I plan to find out tonight.*

"Now," Jewel started, "can we forget about Mr. Weng and Statewide Insurance and my wrecked car? I want to see this beautiful property."

When Taye casually placed an arm across Jewel's shoulders and guided her across the lawn, she was tempted to lean against him, tuck her head down on his shoulder and savor the feel of his body close to hers. How great was it to be alone with him, out of the city and away from prying eyes? The sight of him pleased her in a way she hadn't expected and it struck Jewel right away that she felt more relaxed with him than ever before.

Cutting her eyes at Taye, Jewel focused on his lips and imagined placing hers to his in a quick impulsive peck, just to let him know how happy she was to be there with him. But of course, she wasn't about to express how much she'd missed him or reveal that she'd been thinking about him all day. He seemed very comfortable in this rugged country setting, resembling a cowboy who'd just walked off a movie set in his worn, faded jeans, boots covered with desert dust and a cowboy hat that was stained and bent and so well-worn it could never fit anyone but him. However, his blue-and-white-checkered shirt was crisply starched and ironed, presenting an oddly attractive counter to his otherwise rough-and-tumble appearance. Although tempted to reach up and caress his chin with her hand, Jewel decided it would be best to keep things cool. After all, this was supposed to be a work-related situation and their boss was on his way.

"Can I see the house?" she asked, breaking the silence.

"Of course," Taye agreed, maneuvering Jewel around to the front porch.

Jewel stepped up and then turned around to look down at

Taye, placing both hands on the railing. Leaning in, she probed, "So, what's the new story line? Why this shift to the country? First you cancel the beach location and put Caprice and Darin in a hotel lobby. Now we're going to a ranch? What's going on, Taye?"

Placing a finger to the side of his mouth, Taye thoughtfully focused on Jewel. "I've been thinking of adding a romantic getaway episode for Caprice and Darin. Now that they've had their nasty argument, they need a getaway to make up. Why not whisk them away from Elm Valley to the countryside? Make Darin feel bad about pressuring Caprice, so he plans this as a surprise. What do you think?"

"Hmm…sounds plausible," Jewel replied, running a finger over the rough pine rail. "But what does Lori think? Has she written any of this?"

Instead of answering Jewel's question, Taye mounted the steps and joined Jewel on the porch, where he extended an arm and swept it toward the front door. "Hmm, don't worry about her. She's on board. Now, how about a tour? I'd like your reaction to the setting before we discuss anything else."

"Well, okay," Jewel vaguely replied and then added, "But what about Fred? Think we ought to wait for him so you won't have to do the grand tour twice?"

Taye shrugged, seeming unapologetic, one hand on the doorknob as he studied Jewel. "Oh…I forgot. Fred isn't coming. It'll be just you and me."

"Just you and me, huh?" was all Jewel decided to say about Taye's not-so-subtle plot to be alone with her.

So, here I am, out in the desert, at some stranger's ranch, without my own transportation, stuck with Taye Elliott. Shouldn't she get angry as hell, refuse to step inside the house, demand that he call that limo driver and order him to come pick her up? Yes, she should. But she also knew she was flattered by this bold move, curious about the ranch and impressed that Taye would go to such elaborate lengths to spend time alone with her. As much as she wanted to wrap her arms around his neck and devour those lips, she also knew she had to play it cool. He'd started this game and she was going to play it to the end…whatever that might bring.

"Sorry Fred can't join us," she replied in a flat tone, going along with Taye. As she moved past him and entered the house, the heat from his body seemed nearly as intense as the heat from the bold desert sun.

"Oh my God! I'm impressed," Jewel shouted, stunned by the richly appointed, western-themed interior that greeted her. It had obviously been lovingly created by someone who appreciated the beauty of the west. There was nothing crude about the decor of the lodge, which boasted gleaming hardwood floors throughout the great room where bold Indian rugs divided the space into intimate groupings of distressed leather furniture. The walls were made of chinked exposed logs and covered with oversize oil paintings of western landscapes, pioneer settlements, Indian villages and vivid renditions of early ranch life. Knotty pine tables and hide-covered chairs invited people to sit in front of a natural stone fireplace that covered one wall from the floor to the ceiling.

"This room is beautiful!" Jewel gushed, realizing that it did indeed have real possibilities as a location shoot. She wandered over to a glass-front bookcase and studied the collection, which included many early editions of Zane Gray, Tony Hillerman and classic authors. "The owner has good taste in reading," she stated in appreciation, tensing when Taye stepped up behind her and reached over her shoulder to remove a book from the shelf. His lemon-lime scent sent her pulse racing, initiating an urge to turn around and kiss him.

"Yeah. Lots of good reading here," Taye agreed, reaching past her to remove a copy of Longfellow's *The Song of Hiawatha.* "One of my favorites," he said, brushing his hand against her arm while fanning the pages of the book. When he found what he was looking for, he slipped one arm around Jewel's waist and read from passages describing Hiawatha and Laughing Water's wedding. He recited the poem in an intensely seductive manner, mesmerizing Jewel with his modulated interpretation. When he stopped, she gazed at him, glowing with appreciation for the message he was sending, while struggling not to reveal how deeply he had touched her.

"Beautiful," she managed hoarsely.

"I think so, too," he remarked, eyes roaming her face. "Makes me think of you." He dipped his head, kissed her lightly on the lips and then replaced the book on the shelf. When he turned away, Jewel linked her arm through his, a shiver of contentment sliding over her.

"Come on," she laughingly called out, tugging him along. "Show me more."

"Okay," Taye agreed, walking her across the great room. "Let's explore the kitchen, although I doubt Caprice and Darin will do much cooking while they're here."

Jewel chuckled at his joke and followed him into a small but totally modern kitchen that had a brick oven in the wall and a wonderful collection of black iron pots and pans hanging above the stove. From there, they went outside onto the patio and wandered over to the pool, holding hands, having seemed to accept the fact that neither was going to push back on the shift they'd so gently made.

Letting go of Taye's hand, Jewel squatted down to splash her fingers in the blue-green water. "Oh, I'm impressed," she called out. "It's warm!"

"Yeah, the owner likes to swim year round, so he put in a heated pool."

Jewel straightened up and walked with Taye over to the patio where she sat down on the cushy rattan chaise longue. "Who owns this place, anyway? I'll bet whoever it is wants a bundle to rent it to the studio."

Taye joined Jewel on the chaise, stretched out his long legs and then crossed them at the ankles. He studied his boots in silence. "I have a confession…. I own Double Pass," he stated with pride, shifting his eyes at Jewel, teeth clenched, as if anticipating a negative reaction.

Jewel did not disappoint. With a forward jerk, she flipped

her shoulder and stared suspiciously at Taye. It was bad enough that he'd lured her out to this place in the desert, knowing that Fred Warner was not coming. But he'd brought her to *his* house! Under false pretenses? "What? This is *your* ranch?"

"Yep. It sure is…and if the studio ever wanted to film here, it wouldn't cost a dime."

"Taye! You are so wrong!" Jewel pulled back to look into his face. "I knew something was up with this little jaunt to the country. There never was a plan to use this as a location, was there?"

"There *could* be," he calmly hedged, sounding very serious.

"And you never invited Fred to join us, did you?" Jewel bristled.

"I said I might ask him." A pause.

"You implied that he would be here."

"Yeah. Maybe so. Sorry about that," he lamely confessed.

"So you lied by omission?"

Taye nodded. "Guilty as charged."

Jewel bared her teeth in an angry grimace, but then pushed out a sigh and burst into laughter, giving him a smile of resignation, not amusement. This was one determined man! "You're impossible!" She swatted Taye on the arm, really annoyed, but not nearly as angry as she wanted to be. "You made up all that crap about a location shoot to get me out here alone with you?"

His silence was his answer.

"I don't like being played, Taye," Jewel went on, deciding to get serious and press him for more of the truth. "If this is your home, did you live here with your ex-wife?"

Taye flinched and then glared at her as if she'd slapped him. "No! Never! What made you ask a thing like that?"

"Fred told me you were divorced, so I assumed you may have lived here with…?"

"Rona."

"Rona," Jewel repeated. "Well, did you?"

"No. We never lived here. This place is all mine. And I really don't want to talk about that part of my life, if you don't mind. That disappointing time is behind me. My marriage is over. It was the biggest mistake of my life."

"Well, you could have just invited me to your ranch. Been straight up and told me the truth."

"Would you have come if I had?"

"Of course not!"

"I rest my case," he admitted, easing his hand onto her shoulder.

However, Jewel yanked free, a pout on her lips. "Not so fast! Don't start takin' liberties just because nobody's around. I'm here under false pretenses, remember?"

Taye snaked his hand lower, put his arm around her waist, lifted her, then shifted her closer, testing to see if she would pull away. When she didn't, he gently kissed the side of her neck.

Jewel melted. Her insides turned to liquid fire. All she wanted was for him to ease her down onto the grass and kiss her until she forgot how mad she ought to be.

"There's nothing false about the way I feel about you," Taye breathed against her skin.

His breath felt warm and urgent, dissolving the tension that had been building inside Jewel since she got out of the limo. Here they were, alone, secluded, private, where no one would ever know what they did. The perfect opportunity to let go of every apprehension that had been holding her back. Leaning her head back, she closed her eyes, her body tingling with each kiss that Taye placed along her throat.

"So, what'da you think about my ranch?" he murmured, tickling her with his nose.

"Beautiful. Wonderful. Serene," she murmured as she outlined the lobe of his ear with her finger, her need for him pounding in her blood.

"Just like you," he said, sending a wave of pure joy through Jewel. "You are beautiful, wonderful, serene." His teeth grazed the neckline of her sweater as his tongue flicked over her skin.

Jewel tucked her bottom lip under her front teeth and held her breath, knowing she was drowning in a pool of throbbing desire. "Where do you think we can really take this, Taye? Where's this gonna lead?" She had to ask, wanting to hear him

tell her where they were headed, even though she had no intention of turning back now.

"To wherever you want to go, Jewel." Taye cradled her in
the circle of his arms, her head against his chest as he spoke
above her head. "I'm crazy about you. I mean it. And I'm
willing to do whatever you want. We can take it slow. Take it
fast. Keep it secret or let the world know. I don't care...just tell
me what will make you happy."

His request sent an explosion of possibility through Jewel.
His willingness to compromise had caught Jewel off guard.
He'd shifted the situation into her control and now it was up to
her to decide what would happen next. No matter what she said
or did, she could not deny that she wanted more than hugs and
kisses from Taye Elliott, but was she ready to make such a leap?

A long sigh before she spoke. "Taye, remember when you
promised never to make me feel uncomfortable on the set?"

His fingers worked the buttons on her sweater as he
answered. "I do and I won't. But...first of all, we're not on the
set, so you have nothing to worry about. And second, I think
this seat is pretty damn uncomfortable."

A snicker of agreement from Jewel and then, "What do
you suggest?"

"That," Taye softly continued, "we move inside to a spot I
guarantee would be much better." He opened her sweater,
cupped one breast beneath her bra, his thumb working overtime
on her hard, aching nipple.

What was he asking? To go into his bedroom? To take this
all the way? Jewel shivered at the prospect, her body screaming for more than his touch on her breast, her soul yearning for
shock waves of pleasure to rip through her like thunder. "Well,"
she managed to whisper, turning in his arms to tangle her
fingers in his black curly hair. "You do have very long legs and
this chaise is a bit crowded...."

"Then let's solve the problem right now," Taye decided,
scooping Jewel up in his arms, covering her mouth with his.

She sank into him without resistance, her soul bursting with the prospect of surrender. A moan of pleasure slipped from her lips as she clung to him while he carried her into the house, through the great room and into the master suite, where he placed her down on his king-size bed, which was covered with a soft brown velvet spread.

What am I doing? Jewel worried, searching Taye's features as he eased her sweater over her head. *Am I sure about this? Or am I leading him on?* she fretted, raising her hips to help him remove her khaki slacks. *Why don't I just get up, run away?* she plotted. *But where would I go? Out into the desert? Into the brush like a scared jackrabbit?*

No, she told herself. If she ran, he'd come after her, find her and she'd willingly follow him back to his bed, which was where she knew she wanted to be.

When Taye kicked off his boots, ripped off his shirt and shed his jeans, Jewel let her mind spin forward until nothing mattered but the erotic anticipation sweeping over, pushing her desire to new heights.

She wanted him more than she had ever wanted any man, so what was wrong with having him? They were both grown, free and in control of their lives. Why not let this man make love to her? Why not give in and stop this crazy dance that they'd been doing since they met?

Taye leaned low over Jewel and captured her eyes with his. She groaned and arched her back when he sank his head down between her breasts and suckled each nipple to the point of making her scream.

When he gently spread her legs and eased his hand between them, Jewel raised her hips and rocked her pelvis back and forth, desperate to engage his touch, enjoying the feel of his probing fingers as they stroked and soothed her flaming flesh. His erotic massage pressed urgently into her core, working her to a fever pitch of need until she was totally aroused, craving for Taye to be inside her, and wanting it more than anything in the world.

Reaching for his erection, she stroked his shaft, knowing she had placed herself in this outlandish but delicious position and that she was fully responsible for whatever came next. Sinking fast under his heated touch, her mind swirled with possible ways to end it before it went too far. *I could push him away, laugh this off, call it a teasing rehearsal for my next love scene with Darin. I could tell him I was testing his direction to find out how far he thought he could make me go. Or admit that I need his coaching and want him to show me how to please him.*

However, Jewel didn't say any of those things as her fingers ran the length of his member and his thumb rotated her pulsing clitoris, bringing them both so near to the edge of explosion that there could be no turning back.

When Jewel felt Taye enter her silky, tender core, a shudder of pleasure ripped through her body and escaped as a moan of delight. She thrust her pelvis upward, back and forth, feeling him plunge deeper and deeper inside her as they found a rhythm that suited them both and settled into their erotic journey.

Jewel braced her arms around Taye's shoulders, shaken by the power of her arousal, and not sorry about breaking her long-standing vow to keep such a thing from happening. Falling for her director might be a huge mistake, but Jewel knew she'd find a way to reconcile having the man who shone the spotlight on her desire with keeping her heart and her career intact. *Somehow,* she would manage.

Chapter 19

The next morning, Jewel awoke naked, wrapped securely in Taye's arms, feeling slightly disoriented but content. She lay very still and listened to him breathing softly in her ear while she focused on a magnificent bronze statue of wild mustangs that was sitting on Taye's dresser. Everything about his bedroom was solid, strong and masculine. Like Taye Elliott, she decided. He represented the epitome of rugged male strength. A man's man who made no excuses about it.

Jewel snuggled closer to Taye, bumping her hips against his hard muscular thigh and loving the way it felt. When he suddenly turned and reached for her, she let out a small scream, and then giggled as his hands roamed tenderly over her body, down to caress the spot between her legs that was still wet and hot and eager for more of what he'd given her last night. She had no regrets about the sensual excursion they'd taken until nearly dawn and was eager to take off again.

The California sun was blazing overhead when Taye turned off the grill and removed the Mexican sausage he'd prepared while Jewel was in the kitchen making huevos rancheros and a pot of strong chicory coffee. After having fed each other's sexual appetites until nearly noon, they'd emerged from Taye's bedroom starving for real food.

After breakfast on the patio, they remained outside, leisurely soaking up the sunshine and drinking champagne mimosas with their feet dangling in the blue-tiled Jacuzzi hot tub.

Sipping their drinks with their toes immersed in the bubbling warm water, they shared stories of their early days in Hollywood, of how each had come to this point in their careers and talked about how well things were going on the set of *The Proud and the Passionate.*

"We can't jinx *P & P,*" Jewel remarked, splashing the water gently with her foot as she swept it back and forth.

"We won't. It's gonna be all right. I just hope you're not sorry about last night," Taye replied, not liking the pensive mood in her.

"No, I'm not. I know the risk we're taking," she replied, giving him a wary look.

"So do I," Taye concurred.

Last night had been an incredible, magical experience that he hoped they'd repeat again and again. He had never felt so emotionally and physically connected to any woman before and the sensation was one he embraced, even though he was not so naive as to believe there wouldn't be complications. Soon enough, he'd have to tell Jewel that the ranch was up for sale, that his soon-to-be ex-wife had him in a bind and that he wasn't yet free to make permanent romantic plans.

The thought of strangers sleeping in the bedroom he'd just shared with Jewel or of anyone other than the two of them sitting on the patio on a sunny Sunday morning bothered Taye almost as much as his worry about telling Jewel he was not divorced. He planned to bring up that subject only once—when could tell her his divorce had been granted. Until then, why drag her into his messy struggle to put Rona into his past? It was about to happen any day and he wasn't going to jeopardize what he had found with Jewel by going in that direction. For now, he didn't want to think about any of that. All he wanted to do was enjoy the remainder of their time alone.

While lying in bed with Jewel after making love to her, he'd listened to her talk about her unfortunate relationship with Chandler Jeffries and how miserable she'd been when he broke her heart. He'd sympathized with her distress over having been so publicly embarrassed, hounded by the paparazzi and threatened by Chandler's wife. Taye now better understood why Jewel had adopted her rule of not dating anyone connected to her career. After falling into such a frightening depression, it was no wonder she'd resisted getting romantically involved with him—the man who directed her every move on the set. He hoped she believed him when he told her that he would never hurt her or let her down.

Jewel looked up at Taye with a tentative smile. "No. I'll never be sorry about loving you, even though I know this is crazy." She turned and kissed him lightly on the lips. "Last night couldn't have been more perfect and I don't regret it at all. In fact, I'm more relaxed than I've been in a long time. I feel as if a huge weight has been lifted. Denying my attraction to you was making me so nervous."

"I'm glad the tension's gone," Taye said. He set down his champagne glass and reached out to Jewel, who placed her head on his chest. "I've been worried about you. That's one of the reasons I wanted to bring you out here…to help you forget about work…to focus on your needs."

"How did you know what I needed?" Jewel softly inquired. "How did you know that getting away from the city and away from my problems would make me realize how much I wanted you?"

Taye chuckled and stroked her hair with a calming touch, hoping to ease any anxiety or regrets she might still have. "Instinct. That's a director's secret weapon, you know? To anticipate his actors' needs and push them to discover how to deal with them." Taye hoped Jewel realized how serious he was and how much he wanted her to trust him with her heart.

"Okay, Mr. Know-It-All. What do I need right now?" Jewel

teased, lifting her cheek from his shoulder to show him a mischievous grin.

Taye tilted his head to one side and squinted at Jewel as if pondering her request. "Oh, well. It's nice to hear you asking for *my* direction."

She forced a scowl and rolled her eyes.

"What I think you need..." he started and then without warning, gave her a quick shove, sending her, fully clothed, into the water. "Is a dip in the hot tub!" he finished.

"Taye! That was mean!" Jewel sputtered when she surfaced, shocked by what he'd done. "Look at me! My clothes are totally soaked."

"So, take 'em off." He laughed, standing up to strip off his T-shirt and yank down his jeans, under which he was wearing neither boxers nor briefs. Jumping into the hot tub with Jewel, Taye covered her mouth with his while his hands worked feverishly to remove her ruined sweater and push down her slacks.

"You are absolutely wild!" Jewel complained in the weakest of protests, flinging water from her hair.

Taye held Jewel by her shoulders as she wrapped her legs around his hips. He braced her against the cool blue tile as she centered herself over him. He plunged into her with a determined possessiveness that made him shudder, pushing her until she moaned so loud he feared his neighbors five miles down the road would hear her pleasure-filled cry.

Chapter 20

"Picture up!"
   "Rolling!"
   "Sound speed?"
   "Check."
   "Action!"

Jewel moved into the scene's fifth take, her confidence shaken, unsure of her lines. She was worried, certain that the internal struggle roiling inside would erupt and make her lose all control.

Jewel now realized that she'd been naive to think it would be easy to step into the spotlight Monday morning with Taye's eyes riveted on her, assessing her every move through the lens of their sexual encounter instead of the camera. She'd been foolish to believe it would be possible to separate what they'd shared at his ranch with what they had to share at the studio every day.

After driving Jewel back to Los Angeles late Sunday night, Taye had agreed with her that they simply had to keep their affair secret until Taye's contract ended. The last thing either of them wanted was to lose the trust and respect of their colleagues.

With cameras rolling, Jewel made it through the scene, determined to block Taye out of her mind and focus on her lines.

As the day rolled on, Jewel found the strength to tamp down her emotions and summon a cool facade by limiting her interactions with Taye to necessary responses to his direction. Between takes, she either went to her dressing room or surrounded herself with cast members, blocking any opportunity for Taye to drift over and talk to her. She was more tense, nervous and on guard than before, playing an emotional game of hide-and-seek that she could not afford to lose.

By the end of the week, she was exhausted. When Taye texted her and begged her to go to the ranch with him for the weekend, she agreed without a second thought.

As soon as they arrived at their private getaway, they made love with passionate intensity. Afterward, lying naked in Taye's arms and listening to a Natalie Cole CD, Jewel felt like a contented kitten, all warm and soft and safe. As he traced his tongue and his hands over every inch of her sleek body, she felt him penetrate her soul. This was where she wanted to be, where she belonged.

Over the weekend, they went horseback riding into the mountains, swam in the cool blue pool and enjoyed life in their protected shelter. Away from the prying eyes of coworkers and the threat of paparazzi, they slipped into an easy routine. They shared spontaneous kisses and caresses whenever and wherever they wanted. They laughed while they cooked together, preparing meals to share while they drank wine and talked for hours. They created a world of comfortable companionship, fused by love and protected from the kind of overexposure they both knew could doom them before their love had a chance to blossom.

For Jewel, Taye was the man she'd unknowingly longed for, a man who could fit into her life with little effort. And as soon as his temporary assignment with *P & P* ended, she planned to go public and let everyone know about the happiness she'd found.

Chapter 21

How could Jewel possibly concentrate on kissing Sonny Burton when her mind was consumed with Taye Elliott? All she could think of was how Taye liked to cradle her head with one hand while lowering his lips to hers. How he met her gaze with his deep brown eyes filled with fire-hot yearning. How his tight, hot body melted into hers when their naked flesh impacted.

Jewel's dialogue with Sonny in their bedroom scenes refused to roll off her tongue. The tender expressions she'd memorized hours earlier slipped away, only to be found when she pretended to whisper them to Taye. The seductive passion she had easily summoned for the camera in the past now escaped her, making her words sound dull and flat. And as hard as she tried to find her footing in romantic scenes with Sonny, she failed, having lost her ability to create make-believe love to Darin Saintclare after experiencing the real thing with Taye.

"Can't you see how much I…I…" Sonny stopped in mid-sentence, head cocked at an angle as he squinted hard at Jewel.

He waved a hand in front of her face. "Hello? Hey, there. Are you with me, Jewel?"

She blinked away the flood of intimate thoughts that had been sweeping through her mind and studied him in confusion. Damn. She'd dropped another line and missed her cue again. This was not good. Filming was way behind schedule. Taye had warned the cast that he needed one-take shots from everyone to get back on track. And here she was, wasting precious time because she'd allowed herself to be seriously distracted.

"Sorry, Sonny. I spaced out for a minute." Jewel sounded lame, even to her.

"I can see that," Sonny shot back, genuinely irritated and not trying to hide his impatience. He glared past the camera to where Taye was standing and gave his director a questioning shrug, as if to say, *What in the world is going on?*

"Okay. Okay," Taye called out as he advanced from off camera and leaned into the set. "Can we take it from line thirteen, Jewel? This one has to be *the* take, okay? We've been on this scene way too long."

With a flinch, Jewel nodded, took a deep breath and then resumed her mark, determined to keep her mind on what she was doing.

Taye had been very patient with her for the past two weeks, while under pressure to keep filming on schedule. If her performance, or lack of it, continued to make him lose valuable time, he wouldn't be patient for much longer. She couldn't let him, or the cast, or the studio down. Everyone at *P & P* had a stake in ending the season's major story line with a blowout finale that would ratchet up the ratings. If she wanted to protect the show's future as well as her own, she'd better pull herself together and turn out work that would engage the audience, impress the advertisers and please the studio executives.

Reaching back into the reserve of gritty resolve Jewel knew she still had, she delivered the scene with no more mistakes and then sagged with relief when Taye called "Cut! And print."

Relieved to be finished for the day, Jewel gave Sonny a

quick, appreciative hug for being so patient with her and then hurried across the studio while cast and crew scattered. Stepping over bundles of cables that lay like rail tracks all over the floor, she pushed through the double-door exit leading into the maze of corridors that connected the sound stages to the front lobby. As she turned a corner in a deserted hallway that snaked behind the *P & P* set, she heard Taye calling out her name. "Jewel. Wait! Hey, Jewel!"

She turned around and waited as he approached.

"Wanted to tell you…good job with that final take."

"Thanks," she murmured, sensing his concern, though appreciative of his support. She had made his work today a lot harder than it had to be. "Sorry I took so long to get it right." A beat. "Taye…this is hard. I feel so, so *watched*." She frowned, worried, wishing she could step into his arms and allow him to hold her, comfort her, bolster her unsteady confidence.

A hesitant smile eased over Taye's lips, but he made no move to touch her. Accepting her apology with a nod and a smile, he replied, "Maybe you're trying too hard," he observed. "Forget about me. Act as if I am not there."

"I can't."

"You've got to, Jewel. Don't you see? By blocking me, you're blocking your emotions. Nothing's coming across. Keep it natural, fluid, as you always have, and the lines will flow like they should."

Inclining her head, she stared at the floor. "I'll try."

"Promise?"

She looked up into his eyes, ready to take his criticism in the spirit in which it was offered, knowing he was right. "Yes. I'll get it together, Taye. I will."

"I know you will." He touched her arm then, letting his hand linger for a moment. "I know this is difficult, under these circumstances…but you've got to put me out of your mind. I'm not in the room, okay?"

"That's pretty damn hard," she replied, her heart pounding as her eyes locked with his.

"This isn't easy for me, either. Watching you make love to Sonny Burton is driving me wild and making me pretty damn horny, too."

Jewel slapped playfully at Taye, removing her arm from his hand, feigning a pouty scowl. "Gee, I'm so sorry. Guess you'll just have to suffer in silence until we can be alone."

"When do you think that might be?" Taye prompted.

Jewel smiled, realizing how much just talking to Taye had soothed her ragged nerves. "Tonight? My house. About seven?"

"I'll be there," he murmured. "I can't wait to…"

"Stop it!" she hissed, smothering a laugh. "Please. You are so bad."

"I can't help it. You get to me," Taye confessed with a shrug and a shake of his head. "Anyway, you did fine work today. You just focus on Sonny and everything else will fall into place. The trick is to treat me as if I were Brad Fortune," he suggested with a wink.

"That's asking too much." She lowered her lashes as well as her voice when she boldly stated, "I wasn't in love with Brad."

Taye inched closer, as if to take Jewel in his arms, but she quickly stepped back, lips parted in warning, stirred by the longing in his eyes. Her confession had caught him by surprise and her, as well. She hadn't meant to say those words, but now that they'd been blurted out, she wasn't sorry. She loved him. And the idea of loving him forever sent her spirits soaring. Jewel steadied her breathing, her revelation still hanging in the air, while she wished they were anyplace other than standing in a hallway at CBC trying to keep their hands off each other.

"I'm glad you said that," Taye admitted, his eyes boring into her with steady expectation. "You know I feel the same way, don't you?"

"I was hoping."

"It's true."

"So, now that *that's* out there, what're we gonna do?" she softly questioned, tensing with nervous relief.

However, before Taye could answer, footsteps sounded

farther down the corridor, interrupting their encounter. Jewel quickly backed away. "Gotta go."

"Where're you off to?" he asked, voice much louder and more impersonal, too. A cameraman passed by and gave them a choppy wave of hello.

"I'm on my way to meet with my attorney. About the insurance settlement, remember? Statewide has agreed to a payoff and I'm shocked by the amount. Huge, six figures! I've gotta discuss this with a lawyer."

"You're right about that," Taye said. "But at least it's almost over."

"Really. This is one mess I truly don't need."

"I'm sure it'll go okay. Anyway, I've got that production meeting with Fred and the execs at five, then I'll meet you at your house. Pray the meeting doesn't run too late," he told Jewel, not moving as she backed away.

"Don't worry. I'll have chilled martinis waiting. Call me when the meeting breaks up," she said and then turned around and headed toward the lobby where the car she had called for was waiting outside.

Chapter 22

Even though Jewel's Lexus had been repaired and returned to her a week ago, she continued to use a car service when she didn't feel like driving. Fighting L.A. traffic was not something Jewel missed, and as she slipped into the town car, she couldn't help but smile. Carmie had been right: giving up control over driving had brought Jewel a sense of freedom, not the dreaded dependence she had once imagined. Letting go of that misguided belief had also forced Jewel to reexamine some of the other rules she'd relied on to shape her life and career, and in the process she'd discovered that letting down her guard and allowing herself to love Taye Elliott was the best move she'd ever made.

Half an hour after leaving CBC, Jewel was sitting in the waiting area of Ruth Hardwick's office, anxious to find out what the attorney had to say. She checked her watch for the second time and then settled back in her chair trying to display an ease she didn't particularly feel. The tight muscles in her stomach were due as much to her eagerness to put this accident drama behind her as to the fact that Taye had confessed his love for her. What effect would this have on their relationship? Jewel wondered, brimming with anticipation to see him again. In just a few hours, they'd be at her house, alone, and poised to enter a new, more serious stage of their relationship. She could hardly wait.

In an effort to block out the conversation of two women who were sitting behind Jewel, and obscured by a low plant-filled room divider, she picked up a past issue of *Newsweek* and flipped the pages. However, she was unable to read a word, and while leafing through the publication, she couldn't help but overhear what one of the women said.

"After we leave Saks, we've gotta go to Simply Delicious for dinner," the woman said with great urgency. "You must try their divine shrimp curry. Best I've ever tasted."

"Now, where is it again?" her companion wanted to know.

"North Hollywood. Remember, I told you that my good friend and neighbor, Rona Elliott, owns it. You remember her. She's Taye Elliott's wife. The stunt actor. I think you met her about a year ago…when we were at the club after playing tennis."

Jewel's heart did a solid flip. Her fingers froze on the magazine page. *Did that woman just say Taye Elliott's wife?* She was tempted to turn around and see who they were, but didn't want to appear nosy, and surely didn't want them to recognize her.

"Oh, yeah," the woman's companion remarked. "I do remember her. A pretty girl, but a bit chatty as I recall. I was shocked by how much she revealed about her marriage to Taye, and all their problems. Ruth is her attorney, too."

Jewel jerked forward, eyes narrowed suspiciously. Certainly they couldn't be talking about *her* Taye Elliott. The man she loved. The man she planned to have in her life forever.

"Maybe so," the first woman remarked. "But you gotta give her credit. Rona's smarter than she sounds. She's not about to let that hunky stunt man husband of hers go until she gets exactly what she deserves. He's directing now…making big bucks. She's got a good thing. Why let that go?"

"Hmm…" one woman murmured, sounding sympathetic. "All I remember is her yapping about her messy property settlement…something about a ranch?"

"Right. And truthfully, I feel sorry for her. Rona's had a tough time getting what she deserves from Taye, but either she'll get it, or Taye Elliott will remain married to her for a long time. That girl is one tough cookie who never gives up."

The women's words slammed into Jewel like hammer hits to her heart, beating away at its fragile shell. Flinching, she curled one hand into a tight-fisted ball, pressing it closed until her fingernails cut into her palms and distracted her from breaking into tears. *Taye can't still be married. He's divorced.* She forced her mind back to snippets of past conversations she'd had with Taye, letting them tumble around in her mind as she struggled to sort this news out. *I asked him about his marriage during my first visit to the ranch. He didn't want to elaborate on it. He called his marriage the biggest mistake of his life. He sounded so sincere. I dropped the subject, thinking it must be a painful chapter in his life that he did not want to discuss. Why didn't I press the issue?*

"Rona's got grit," the woman with the higher-pitched voice was saying. "But right now, she sure is in a messy situation. Good luck, is all I can say."

Jewel's heart was beating so fast she could feel it pounding erratically under her blouse and hoped she didn't look as anxious as she felt. An unfamiliar sense of doom began to creep in and she didn't like the feeling. Jewel's mind spun and her stomach lurched while all the air in the room seemed to vanish, making it difficult to breathe. She suddenly felt so off balance she had to grip the arms of her chair for support.

"Miss Blaine?" Ruth Hardwick's cool-voiced receptionist called out, jerking Jewel alert. "Ms. Hardwick will see you now."

Jewel, whose ears were still ringing from what she'd overheard, stood and managed to walk on shaky legs into the attorney's office.

After taking a seat, Jewel handed Ruth the fax that Statewide

Insurance had sent her, and while the attorney reviewed the proposed settlement, turned her attention to the numerous certificates and degrees that were framed and hanging on the wall behind Ruth, desperate to distract her thoughts from what she'd just overheard. All Jewel wanted right then was for Ruth to help her make the accident ordeal go away, so that she could concentrate on digging out the truth about Taye Elliott's marital status.

Had he lied to her? Deliberately misled her? Taken her for a fool? It was all Jewel could do to keep from breaking into tears.

"I think it's a fair offer," Ruth Hardwick finally stated, bringing Jewel back to the moment.

"Really?" Jewel managed, both relieved and disturbed.

"Yes. I think so." Ruth removed her gold-rimmed glasses and set them on her desk blotter. Leaning back in her executive chair, she pursed her lips in thought. "I know you don't like this, Jewel, but settling out of court is the best way to go. Statewide is not going to invest the time and expense required to fight this, so my advice is…let it go."

"I see your point," Jewel said, nodding. "But it still seems so unfair. Those men were not injured, and Mr. Weng knows that. He drove away on his own!"

Ruth shook her head in resignation. "Maybe so, but why fight over that? Statewide is offering them a nice hunk of change and they've stated that your policy premiums won't increase. That's extremely important. Besides, it would be costly for you to try to prove the men weren't injured, and I doubt you want to go that route. Don't forget, this consultation is on the house. I get enough work from CBC to help you out with this."

Jewel sat back, feeling defeated but ready to surrender. She'd come to Ruth Hardwick for her advice and she'd gotten it. Now, it was time to move on to tackle a new set of problems. "Think the Wengs will accept the offer?" Jewel wanted to know.

"If they don't, then it'll have to go to court and they'd probably get a much lower judgment. They'll take it, I guarantee," Ruth replied. "If the Wengs accept Statewide's settlement, this can be over, Jewel. I know you wished it hadn't happened like this, but that's what you pay insurance premiums for. Protection. Now, anything else on your mind?" Ruth asked, slipping the fax from Statewide into a folder, which she put on top of a stack to be filed.

If you only knew, Jewel thought, having made up her mind about what she had to do.

After hurriedly thanking Ruth Hardwick for her help, Jewel made a fast exit and got into her Town Car.

"Do you know where a restaurant called Simply Delicious is?" she asked the driver, leaning over the front seat.

"Sure do. It's a popular spot. Not far." He started the engine and put the car into Drive.

"Take me there," Jewel stated. It was time to pay Rona Elliott a visit and get the truth from the source.

Chapter 23

In the car on her way home, Jewel was so agitated she could hardly sit still and was thankful she wasn't driving. She wanted to tell the driver to take her back to the studio, so she could march into Taye's meeting and demand that he come to her dressing room, where she'd tell him exactly what a jerk he was for toying with her like this. She wanted to slap his face, hurt him, make him sorry he'd ever attempted to romance her and then walk away from *P & P,* leaving him hanging out there with no star to direct.

Jewel gave up a harsh laugh. That would really fix him! She had the power to turn his daytime directorial debut into a true disaster. Hell, *Down for Love* wanted Jewel Blaine. She could walk off the set of *P & P* and join the cast of *DFL* tomorrow if she wanted to and the thought brought a wicked smile to her lips. For the first time in her career she was actually considering breaking her contract at CBC.

She grabbed her phone and then checked her watch. Twenty minutes after five. The production meeting had already begun. Her confrontation with Taye would have to wait. *Until he gets to my house. Where we can be alone. Where I can really let him have it.*

Going limp, she ratcheted down her anger by holding her breath and counting to twenty. She stared glumly out the car window, plotting their confrontation, looking forward to show- ing Taye Elliott exactly who was in charge of their show.

When Jewel's cell phone rang, she peered at the screen and then flipped it open to greet her agent with a snippy, "Hello, Marlena! What do you want?"

"Wow. Maybe I should hang up and call later?" Marlena shot back, cautiously surprised.

Jewel sagged back in her seat, ashamed. "No, no. I'm sorry. I've got a lot on my mind right now."

"As I assume you did last Sunday?"

"Sunday?" Jewel repeated, trying to get her bearings. Sun- day seemed so long ago, as if it had come and gone in a dream. A time when she had let down her guard and trusted Taye with her heart, putting faith in him, which he obviously didn't deserve.

"We had a brunch date for eleven-thirty at Piatto's, remem- ber?" Marlena was saying. "This is the second time you've stood me up."

"Oh, damn. I completely forgot to call you back."

"That's right. I called you twice. So you did get my messages?"

"Yes, I did," Jewel confessed. "But I've been…busy. Well, out of town, really."

"Yeah? Where'd you go?"

Groping for what to say, how much to reveal, and frightened by the tears building behind her eyes, Jewel's voice shook as she told Marlena, "I was at… Okay. At Taye's ranch in the San Gabriel Mountains."

"Taye Elliott's ranch?"

"Yes."

"Hmm, sounds interesting." Silence hummed on the line. "You and Taye and…who else?" Marlena skillfully probed.

"No one else. Just the two of us. For the past several

weekends," Jewel divulged, ready to clear the air and get everything out in the open. She needed Marlena's friendship more than ever, without being judged for past mistakes.

"I see," Marlena murmured, before asking, "Wanna talk about it or is the subject off-limits?"

Sucking in a long breath, Jewel pulled herself together enough to spill everything to Marlena, pausing to compose herself between sobs of disappointment. Taye was not the honest, upstanding man she'd thought he was. If he'd been truthful from the start she never would have acted on her attraction to him. What a loser! He'd deliberately misled her, gotten her emotions all tangled up, to the point of jeopardizing her career. How had she allowed her love life to get so far off-course—again?

What if his soon-to-be ex was holding out for a reconciliation? What if she stalled the proceedings for years? Jewel trembled, afraid of spiraling into the emotional wreck she'd become once before, terrified of returning to that awful state of being insecure, adrift and alone with her regrets.

"Sounds pretty simple to me," Marlena finally stated in her wise, maternal tone after Jewel stopped talking. "You're in love, but you've convinced yourself that Taye isn't worth fighting for. Otherwise, you'd be on the phone talking to him instead of me. Am I close?"

A long silence before Jewel answered, "Maybe." She sniffled and swallowed hard. "I do love him, but I can't get over the fact that he lied to me!"

"Did he actually tell you he was divorced?"

Jewel opened her mouth to snap back in the affirmative, but stopped, her mind whirling back to the only conversation they'd had about his marriage. He'd told her that his marriage was over, that he'd put the disappointing experience behind him. Fred Warner was the one who'd told Jewel that Taye was divorced and she had taken him at his word.

Marlena pressed her case. "I take your silence to mean no?"

"Okay. He didn't spell it out."

"So, don't go charging the guy up about lying," Marlena

advised. "Withholding vital details does make him come off like a total jerk, but if the man honestly loves you and you love him, be careful. Don't blow it, Jewel. Talk to him. Make him tell you exactly what's going on and then you can decide where to go from there."

As angry, disappointed and ashamed as Jewel was, she knew Marlena had a point. This was the man she had trusted with her career, her heart, her future. The man who made her feel loved, secure and alive. She wouldn't trash their relationship without first giving Taye a chance to explain why he'd put her in this deceitful situation and Jewel would reserve the right to believe him or not.

Chapter 24

"Come on in, Taye. Have a seat." Fred Warner motioned to the empty chair across from him at the conference table, where Richard Young, the head of advertising at CBC, and Art Freeman, head of programming, were poring over sheets of paper spread out in front of them. "The weekly ratings roundup is in. Doesn't look too good," Warner announced with a grunt as Taye picked up his copy of the latest Nielson Ratings report and began to review it.

Richard Young tapped the table three times with his index finger, looking over the top of his reading glasses. "For the week ending May 8, *Y & R* is up two, *B & B* up one, *GH* up one. And *P & P* is down two. That's huge, Taye. A real stunner. Two weeks into May sweeps and we're dropping like a lead ball tossed in the river. What's happening?"

Instead of allowing Taye to offer an explanation, Fred quickly interceded. "We've got fierce competition breathing down our necks, that's what. The other soaps are tearing us a new ass and you know why?"

Taye kept quiet, accustomed to Fred Warner's rhetorical questions.

"Because they pulled out the big guns," Fred went on. "They brought back well-known vets and let bombshell story line revelations push them over the top. Either way you slice it…things are lookin' good for everyone but us."

Taye felt as if he'd been punched in the gut. From the looks on the faces of the people in the room, he knew he had to give them something. But what could he say? That Jewel Blaine was not delivering and it was most likely Taye's fault? That Sonny was nervous because Jewel was off her game and her jittery attitude was affecting her costar? What could he say to these men without revealing the truth—that his love for Jewel was the source of their frustration, including his?

"We got off to a late start, with my replacing Brad and all," Taye began. "But things are beginning to click. I'm sure we'll get a bounce next week with the finale of the story line where Caprice finally gives in and takes Darin back. Lori's rewritten the reunion scene and it's a hell of an explosive bedroom scenario. Sexy, hot…a real meltdown, cliffhanger episode. I'm convinced we're on the right track."

Warner leaned back in his chair, hands crossed on his stomach in a studious manner. "One episode won't create the kind of momentum we need to carry us through to the end of sweeps. You've got to keep it building, Taye. How can we catch up and pass the top five soaps, who got off to a good start and kept the pressure on?"

"That's right," Richard said. "*GH* brought back the heavy hitters by showcasing veteran actors. *Y & R* exploded with the secret of Lily's paternity and then shocked everyone with news that Phyllis is pregnant. *OLTL* went for natural disasters with a torrent of tornadoes. *B & B* put Ridge's life on the line. *AMC* shut down Kendall by putting her in a coma."

"Huge stories…exactly what bumps the numbers," Art Freeman piped up, shaking a finger in the air. "Our ad revenues are down. I've seen this week's dailies and it seems to me that

Caprice and Darin aren't creating the kind of passion they used to. They're acting like a freaking brother-sister team. What's with the strange chemistry between those two?"

The knot in Taye's stomach tightened. He knew exactly what was going on. Hadn't Sonny complained to him about Jewel's performance? And Taye had done nothing about it. He'd watched Jewel through the camera lens and seen how tentatively she was behaving. He'd done take after take on too many scenes not to know she was stumbling through her lines. He knew that *he,* Taye Elliott, had to shoulder most of the blame for this drastic dip in ratings.

"I'll talk to them. We'll pull up," Taye promised, going on to explain in great detail how he planned to turn things around. "Next week *P & P* will be back in the top five. Keep cool, guys, Caprice Desmond won't let her fans down."

Fred coughed under his breath. "I don't know about that. Suzy's been forwarding e-mails to me all week and there've been a substantial number of complaints. Fans want to know where is the feisty Caprice Desmond they used to love. Face it, Taye, Jewel is letting her audience down and we need to find out why."

With a gulp, Taye sucked in the order, knowing his worst fears had come true. Once fans started complaining, the message became clear: whatever was going wrong had spread beyond the studio and he had to fix it—fast. "I will. I'll talk to Jewel, but remember, she had a hard time getting over Brad's death, adjusting to my style. She just needed a little time…"

"In daytime, things move fast," Richard interrupted. "We don't have time to coddle her, Taye."

"Okay, I know…. I'll do what I can to find out what's making her so…so cautious about letting go. I'll talk to her right away."

Leaning over the table, Art locked eyes with Taye. "Good. And for the record, I don't want you to think CBC has lost faith in *you,* but it is the director's job to make sure the actors deliver."

Taye squirmed in his seat, realizing that *P & P's* future, as well as his, was on the line. Deciding to see exactly where things stood, he asked, "I want you to be honest. Am I the wrong director for this show?" He waited, ready to face the truth.

Fred coughed, focusing on Taye. "I don't think these recent ratings are the fault of the director. But—" he paused, chin lowered "—let's be clear. And none of what I am about to say can be repeated outside this room. Understand?"

Taye inclined his head in agreement.

"I think Jewel Blaine is underperforming," Fred said. "I don't know why she's not giving us what we need, but she isn't. However, she is not the entire problem. There're a lot of variables at work here. *P & P* has been slipping for the past two quarters. *Down for Love* is whipping everybody's ass. There was a time when *P & P* was the hottest soap around, but its newness has faded and the intrigue is gone, so fans have moved on. Could be, *P & P* has run its course. And if so, we've got to be smart enough to cut the deadwood and go for something fresh."

Taye bit his bottom lip, but remained silent, taking in Fred's pronouncement.

"However," Fred continued. "We're very pleased with your work, Taye. If *P & P* is canceled, we plan to use your directorial talent in some other venue…if you choose to stick around."

"That's right." Art entered the conversation. "You've got a future at CBC, so don't start worrying about that. If *P & P* doesn't survive, and it might not, *you* definitely will." He adjusted his tie and looked toward the other men, who bobbed their heads and smiled at him, urging him to go on. "Taye, I want to speak bluntly."

"Fine with me," Taye replied.

"African Americans have had a presence in daytime serials for more than forty years, although too often it's been in non-essential roles."

Taye nodded in complete understanding.

"*The Proud and the Passionate* has been successful, but it has also shown us how much further we need to go. There are very few black writers, producers and directors in the so-called 'top echelon' of production, which is where we want to keep you. Taye, you're talented and have what we want. Your job right now is to pump up *P & P*'s story line, show us what you can do. If you bring in respectable numbers for May sweeps, the network has great plans for you."

Taye left the meeting feeling happy, stressed, anxious and even guilty, yet filled with a strange sense of relief about his fate in daytime television. A real mixed bag of messages had been dumped on him, creating a landslide of questions waiting to be answered. Clearly, *The Proud and the Passionate* was on shaky ground and Jewel Blaine might go down with it. However, both Art and Fred couldn't have been more clear: Taye's career at CBC was solid!

As Taye left the building and crossed the parking lot, he struggled to put everything in perspective. If *P & P*'s dip in ratings was a direct result of his secret relationship with Jewel, shouldn't he tell her? Warn her? Break his promise to the execs and give Jewel a heads-up—that the CBC honchos were talking about a possible cancellation of *P & P?*

Taye drove out of the parking lot in a semitrance, unable to think about anything other than the fact that he really should break off with Jewel and put an end to the stress she was under. Or maybe he should quit his job, walk away from CBC and go back to directing indie action flicks, where his life had been much less complicated.

Taye headed to Jewel's house, struggling for answers and fearful that none of the options that were flitting through his mind were plausible solutions. He loved his job. He loved Jewel Blaine. And he wasn't about to give up either. Somehow, he'd make this complicated situation work out for both of them.

Chapter 25

What to wear to a breakup? Something seductive enough to lure Taye into a false sense of anticipation or an outfit so plain and unappealing that it immediately sent the message that their evening together would not end in the bedroom? That was the question surging through Jewel's mind as she shimmied out of a clingy ivory skirt that definitely wasn't working and grabbed her ringing cell phone. Just as she'd thought, it was Taye.

"I'm on my way," he told her as she tossed the skirt on a pile of the other discards from her closet.

"Good. How did the meeting go?" Jewel asked with forced calm, her entire body zinging with the urge to scream at him.

"I wasn't fired," Taye joked. "In fact, Fred seems pleased with my work, so maybe he'll keep me around after sweeps."

God, I hope not, Jewel silently prayed.

"Anyway," Taye went on, "I'll tell you all about it when I get there." A beat. "What about the insurance claim? What did the lawyer say?"

More than you can even imagine, Jewel fumed, tensing the

muscles in her jaw as Ruth Hardwick's revelation flooded back into her brain. Jewel felt as if weights had been attached to her body, slowly pulling her down into a thick pool of mud. Struggling to find her voice, she told Taye, "The attorney thinks Statewide's offer is more than fair and if the Wengs are smart, they won't refuse it."

"Great. Now you can forget about it, okay? Aren't you glad that mess is over?"

Yes, but a new, more horrible one just crashed into my life. Another accident that's all my fault.

"Yeah," Jewel said in a whispery, almost sad voice. "I'm glad it's over. It was stressing me out way too much."

She sat on the edge of her bed and stared at the floor for a long time after saying goodbye, but then gave herself a mental shake and got down to business. Taye was on his way; she had to get dressed and put her plan into action.

After stepping into a pair of skintight black satin pants, she pulled on a red stretch top that revealed precisely the right amount of skin and cleavage. Wild red lipstick, hair piled into a sexy, messy up-do and black leather wedge thongs studded with rhinestones on her feet. A satisfied twirl in front of the mirror and then Jewel headed into the kitchen.

Gotta have music, she decided, turning on her CD player to let Toni Braxton's "Shadowless" spill out and dissolve the silence. Humming along, Jewel opened an upper cabinet and pulled out the gold-rimmed platters and bowls that she kept in pristine condition behind glass doors. *Tonight's dinner is going to be special, so why not use the good stuff?* she mused, pleased with her decision to pick up some takeout instead of having Carmie come over to cook. With great care, Jewel placed satay chicken, jasmine rice, spiced cabbage and steamed vegetable dumplings in delicate serving pieces, adding leaves of cilantro, sliced ginger and bits of green onions as garnish. Satisfied with the presentation, she placed the food on heating trays and set it on the blue cloth she'd tossed over the dining room table.

Standing back, Jewel smiled with approval and then went

into the den where she circled the bar and began setting out the ingredients for apple martinis. Taye's favorite drink. The beverage they'd sipped on the patio at her house, while soaking in the hot tub at his ranch and while cuddling together and talking in bed.

With a jut of her chin, she squashed those memories and began mixing the first batch of martinis. She poured a drink for herself, tasted it and then, with a smack of her lips, nodded. Perfect. With a toss of the glass, she finished it off and poured herself another. *I'm gonna need more than one of these to get through this night.*

While working on the second batch, the doorbell rang. Taye was here! Shoving her nervous anxiety aside, Jewel clenched her teeth in determination, desperate to kill the disappointment and anger that threatened to erupt. Keeping a firm grip on her emotions, she walked into the foyer on stiff, mechanical legs, although her entire body was quivering.

If only he'd told me the truth from the start, we wouldn't be in this situation. I never would have dreamed of a future with him, a future I now have to toss in the trash like yesterday's newspaper. I fell for a man I couldn't trust and risked my career for a man who wasn't even free to love me. Stupid me! But I can't worry about that now. After tonight, Taye Elliott will be history and I'll be back on track.

"Hi," Taye said, stepping inside to kiss Jewel lightly on the lips as soon as she opened the door.

Pulling back, she offered him an innocent smile, gave him a hug and then linked her arm through his and walked him into the den.

"Martinis are ready!" she cheerfully announced in as normal a tone as she could muster. She made sure her eyes were not on him while pouring the green liquid into two martini glasses. After handing one to him, she lifted hers and said, "What should we drink to?" Her tone was teasingly serene, keeping the mood light before the evening deteriorated into the emotional chaos Jewel knew was coming.

"How about to us?" Taye suggested, placing his glass to his lips, preparing to take a sip.

With a tilt of her head and a lift of her chin, Jewel paused, deliberately allowing an expression of sultry intrigue to slip over her features. "Hmm. I dunno about that. How about to the future instead?" she countered, watching Taye for his reaction. "To whatever comes next, whatever that might be."

Grinning, Taye acquiesced with a sexy wink. "You sound awfully mysterious. Intriguing, in fact. You planning something special?"

"You'll find out soon enough," Jewel answered, her features becoming more animated.

Taye clinked his glass to hers. "You've got me. To whatever comes next," he toasted, tilting back his head to drink.

Jewel moved from behind the bar and sat on the stool next to Taye. "So, how'd the meeting with Fred and the studio execs go?" She leaned over, allowing her cleavage to deepen, pleased when Taye's eyes roamed her breasts with open appreciation. Jewel held her breath as a cascade of conflicted emotions ran through her.

God, how she loved this man! He was handsome, sexy and intelligent. Creative, talented and in love with her! They fit together in bed, in play, even at work. He possessed the hands, the tongue, the arms and the perfect erotic tool to sex her to satisfaction and then some. She wanted him in her life, in her heart until the end, and inside her body, urging her higher and higher until her world exploded in quivering gasps of release. But that could not happen as long as he was married and her disappointment in Taye for disregarding the personal and professional consequences of his lie burned in her chest like a flame that wouldn't die.

Now, Jewel struggled to focus on what Taye was saying.

"We mainly discussed *P & P*'s drop in ratings. Not the subject I had hoped to talk about, but that's exactly where we stand, Jewel. At the bottom, going into the last two weeks of sweeps. It's not a good place to be. Either we pull up at least half a point next week or there could be problems."

"Really? That sounds a bit drastic," Jewel countered, placing her glass on the bar where she twirled it around by the stem. "Fred won't let anything happen that could negatively impact *The Proud and the Passionate.* I know that for sure."

"Hey, I was just telling you what I got from Richard and Art," Taye tossed back, going on to talk about what the other soaps were doing to hold on to their ratings share. "I can't give you specifics, Jewel, but I have to say—" He stopped and sucked in a long breath. "Don't let yourself be blindsided. You know the industry. You know what can happen. Watch out for yourself, okay?"

As Taye rattled on, Jewel recalled her conversation with Marlena. *Down for Love* wanted Jewel Blaine for a contract role. Marlena thought Jewel should consider taking it.

Could that be the right move? Jewel allowed herself to question. *I'd get away from Taye Elliott, put an end to my frustrations, be finished with the man who toyed with my heart and broke it.* Jewel knew she hadn't been doing her best work because she was distracted and couldn't concentrate. So, how long could she go on like that, especially after tonight?

"You know what, Taye?" she began, sliding off the stool, wanting to put career discussions aside. She had one thing on her agenda tonight and that was to get Taye Elliott out of her life. "Let's not talk about *P & P,* okay? We don't get that much time alone, so let's put tonight to good use." Hoping her voice hadn't betrayed her motive, she assessed Taye for a moment and then asked, "Hungry?"

"Always," Taye replied. He stood, caught Jewel by the waist, pulled her to him and brushed his lips back and forth against her temple. "And after dinner?" he murmured, sliding lips down to her ear to gently suckle the lobe.

"Wait and see," Jewel teased, easing out of his embrace to tug him by the arm toward the dining room where the food she'd spread out was waiting. "What do you think?" She extended her arm, referring to the food.

"Looks simply delicious," he commented, picking up a plate, spearing a piece of chicken.

Jewel shook out her white linen napkin, which she fanned back and forth over the table, chuckling. "Gee. You're right! That's exactly where all of this wonderful food came from."

Taye stopped, his speared chicken dangling in midair as he jerked around and stared at Jewel. Clearly puzzled, he squinted hard at her. "What did you say?"

Jewel fluttered her eyelashes in innocence, lips slightly parted, wanting to appear absolutely nonplussed even though her heart was breaking. "Oh, I think it's funny, that's all. You said, 'simply delicious.' That's where I bought the food. At a restaurant called Simply Delicious. In North Hollywood. Ever heard of it?"

Taye dropped the forked piece of chicken back onto the platter with a splat. Had he heard Jewel right? Who told her about the restaurant? When?

"I…I dunno. Maybe I've heard of it. Why do you ask?" he stuttered, thinking it best to play this safe until he got his bearings.

"I thought maybe you'd been there for lunch because it's new, not too far from the studio and the food is great."

With a shrug, Taye truthfully replied, "No, I've never been inside the place."

"Hmm…I'm surprised," Jewel murmured as she spooned jasmine rice onto her plate and then fiddled with the spoon in the cabbage.

"Why are you surprised?" Taye asked, suspicious about where this was going, and wanting her to tell him exactly what was on her mind.

"Because Rona Eaton owns Simply Delicious. She *is* your wife, isn't she?"

No way could he reply.

"And I guess I supposed that most husbands love their wives' cooking and enjoy it as often as possible."

Taye froze. Every muscle in his body went into lockdown and his stomach did a nasty flip. Oh God. She knew he was not divorced. Knew he had not been totally truthful with her. "Who's been discussing my personal life with you? Who told you my ex-wife owns a restaurant?"

"*Wife,* you mean! Not ex!" Jewel shouted, ready for a fight.

"Okay, okay. *Almost* ex! But I want to know who's been talking about my personal business."

Jewel's laugh was a nasty snarl. "Let's just say your wife and I share a legal connection."

"Legal? Your attorney? The same as Rona's?"

Jewel grinned and curled her lip in answer, leaving Taye to flounder. The gig was up; he had to come clean and pray she would listen to what he had to say.

"Rona is not my wife. Not in ways that matter. We signed off on our property settlement the day I started working at CBC. It's long been over, Jewel."

"Right. Give me a break!"

"Will you listen to me? I want to tell you everything," he ventured, praying she would understand, not judge him too harshly.

"Why now? You've had plenty of chances to come clean. Why did I have to find out on my own? You really do disgust me."

"I wanted to tell you, but the time was never right."

Jewel slapped her linen napkin against her palm and narrowed her eyes at Taye. "Okay. Talk while I eat, because I am not going to waste all this delicious food. Go ahead. I'm all ears," she shot back in a sarcastic sneer. She reached for a plate and calmly placed a dollop of cabbage on top of her rice.

Taye watched as Jewel continued to fill her plate, taking her time as if nothing was wrong. He had to give her her props for the acting job she was pulling off, because he knew she must be devastated. Why had he been so stupid? Why had he thought he could keep his divorce a secret until it was final? Why had he risked playing out this very scene, which could have been avoided? *Well, here goes,* Taye decided, hating the sinking sensation that roared through him and made him slightly nauseous.

"I know I've got some serious explaining to do," he started, his defenses subsiding. He straightened his shoulders, recapturing control, and started at the beginning. After speaking about how he'd met and foolishly married Rona, he made the mistake of extending a hand toward Jewel, wanting to connect with her as he talked, but she slammed her plate of food down on the table, turned her back on him and stomped into the den, where she flung herself onto the sofa and glared at him with daggers in her eyes.

Taye hurried to a seat next to her, leaned forward, hands dangling between his legs. "I'm serious, Jewel." When she didn't respond, he went on. "Rona is no longer my wife."

"Liar! Don't start by telling me you're *divorced,* because I know you aren't," Jewel snapped, jutting her chin toward the ceiling.

"You're right. Not legally. I can't say that, but we've been separated for nearly two years. That's a long time, Jewel, and the only contact I've had with her has been through our lawyers. When we separated, as far as I was concerned, she no longer existed and I was no longer married to her, even though we've had a nasty property settlement to work out."

"So I heard from Rona," Jewel muttered, arms crossed firmly at her waist, pleased to see the look of surprise that came over Taye's face. Jewel had had an awkward but fruitful conversation with Rona, who had been happy to provide the information Jewel sought, nearly bragging about her intact marital status as Taye's legal wife.

"Right. And as soon as we get a court date, it'll be final. It's been a long, difficult process, but I'm at the end. Really, Jewel. I wanted you to know everything when the time was right. You see, Rona's been fighting me for more and more money, until I had to put the ranch up for sale. If I'd given her Double Pass two years ago, I'd be divorced right now."

"Oh, spare me!" Jewel groaned. "You're okay with staying married to her so you can keep your precious ranch? What an asshole you are, Taye. You'd let me believe you were free to enter into a relationship and you'd covered up the fact that you're still married just to hold on to some land? Please! That is so disgusting."

"But that's not what's happening, Jewel. Rona's restaurant,

which I bankrolled so she'd have a means of support, isn't turning a profit. So, I'm forced to sell Double Pass and give her half."

Jewel laughed openly at that remark. "Surely you don't believe that shit! Your wife's restaurant was sure as hell packed tight when I was there. It was a madhouse. I had to wait nearly an hour for my takeout. And while I was standing around waiting, I chatted with a woman who eats there every day. She said the place is always packed. Constantly. So, if wifey says she's broke, she's playin' you for a jerk because she's really rakin' in the dough."

Taye shrugged off her remark and pressed on. "Any way you cut it, Rona can't support herself and because the ranch is community property, the law says I have to give her half. It's up for sale."

"I've never seen any For Sale signs around there."

"That's because I took them down."

"More deceit."

Taye sighed, resigned to accept that barb. "Maybe so. I hid the signs the first time you came out because I wasn't ready to go into why the ranch was up for sale. Anyway, I still own Double Pass and until it's sold, I have every right to be there. It's mine!"

"You're such an inconsiderate bastard. Taking me on long rides across the desert and talking about your plans for improving the ranch when it's about to be sold! A sham! That's all you are. One great big sham."

"Yes, I love Double Pass. I wanted to believe I could hold on to it somehow. Guess I can't expect you to understand how hard it was for me to give in to Rona's demands and put it on the market. But right now, you know what? I don't want it. Not if it means I can't be free. I want my divorce to be finalized. I want freedom. I want you." His voice cracked with emotion and his heart swelled with longing and for the first time since meeting Jewel, he felt real fear.

Before tonight, he'd worked the situation out in his head, as if blocking out a scene in a movie, scripting the ending he wanted. But this was real life and the story line wasn't playing out as he'd planned. He was no longer the director of this episode and this loss of control was frightening.

"I never planned on hurting you," he confessed. "Guess that's why I avoided talking about my divorce. The delay was dragging me down, Rona was driving me crazy. I sure as hell didn't want to get you tangled up in my problems."

"But you should have been up-front about it!" Jewel launched at him in anger. "Let *me* decide what *I* want to do! How dare you play director with my feelings and try to orchestrate my life? You've got a lot of nerve, making love to me knowing you were still married. But that's what you do, isn't it, Taye? You prod and push and manipulate people until you get them to do exactly what you want…on the set and off. Well, I'm sorry I fell for that trap."

"Jewel, please. I never deliberately manipulated you. Hell, I never planned on falling in love with you, either. And yes, I plead guilty to masking the truth, but I did it out of love for you…to protect you from Rona, who can be tough to deal with when she doesn't get what she wants. I didn't want you to be named in my divorce action, for you to be dragged into court and my messy divorce. I know what you went through once before and I wanted to protect you from anything like that."

"Gee, thanks, but your kind of protection, I don't need."

"All I want is a future with you."

"Which we definitely will never have," Jewel threw back with a snap. She stood, strode to the front door and yanked it open. "You'd better go." A crude, sarcastic laugh erupted when she told Taye, "Exit, please, Mr. Director. This is the final act of our story."

Taye bristled at the finality of her statement, knowing there was nothing to do but leave. What point was there in trying to smooth things over after destroying her trust in him? He'd blown it. He'd messed up. Big-time.

As Taye walked past Jewel, he could not stop himself from reaching out to touch her arm in goodbye and wasn't surprised when she flinched and jerked away. However, he was surprised when she murmured, "I'm sorry it's ended like this, Taye."

He paused and studied her face for a long moment, captivated anew by her beauty, struck by the deep regret he saw shining through the tears that glistened in her luminous brown eyes.

Driving home, Taye blinked back his own tears, determined not to lose control. Jewel had every right to be furious with him. He'd have felt the same way if some man held legal claim to her. *She needs space, time and reassurance that my love for her is rock solid. But I don't have a chance in hell of getting her back until I'm legally free.* But when would that be? What did he need to do?

Chapter 26

Friday night passed in a blur of moody silence, rage-filled out-bursts and weepy crying jags that came over Jewel without warning, followed by loud self-talk as she paced her empty house and chastised herself for allowing this to happen. Cursing, sobbing and plotting her next move, she tried to fathom the future.

What if Taye stayed on as the permanent director of *P & P?* No question but she'd have to quit the show! Maybe she should call Fred right then and tell him she was through! Or wait until Monday and walk off the set in the middle of a scene, leaving Mr. Taye Elliott high and dry. That would throw a roadblock in his triumphant daytime debut.

Perhaps she should call Marlena, go after that role at *Down for Love.* Take her fans and her talent to a director who would treat her with respect, not manipulate her for his personal pleasure.

But Jewel was too paralyzed with disappointment to take any kind of action. Instead, she pulled into herself, blocked out the world and slipped into a frightening depression that left her angrier and more disappointed than she'd been after the Chandler Jeffries affair.

On Saturday morning, when Carmie arrived to work on Jewel's fan mail, Jewel told her she'd changed her mind and didn't need any help after all. She had a headache, wasn't in the mood to deal with anything remotely connected to work and wanted to be left alone. She should have known Carmie wouldn't be so easily put off and it didn't take much prodding for Jewel to spill her story between sobs of self-pity and outbursts of anger.

"I'm glad it's over," Jewel confessed to Carmie, lifting her jaw with a resolute turn of her head. "I don't need him, never did. I should have seen through him the first day. All talk and show. Nothing real about him at all. My fans and my work are all I need."

"Hmm," Carmie grunted, reaching for a stack of letters. She ripped open a piece of fan mail. "Quit trying to fool me and yourself. Why can't you admit that you love that man?"

"Oh? How do you know so much?" Jewel tried to tease, uncomfortable with Carmie's remark.

"I just do," Carmie stated flatly, leaving no room for discussion. "You're in love. So, want my advice? Think about forgiving him or get ready to see some other woman on his arm, flashing a satisfied smile."

Jewel playfully slapped Carmie on the arm with an empty envelope. "I'm hardly worried about that. Go on back home and enjoy the rest of your weekend, okay? I just want to be alone."

After Carmie left, Jewel's defenses collapsed. Tears rolled unchecked as she thought about her assistant's advice. Was Carmie right? Did Jewel love Taye enough to forgive him? Did she need Taye Elliott back in her life?

By Sunday, Jewel had calmed down enough to stop thinking about herself and to turn her thoughts to Taye. How was he handling the breakup? Was he as lost and hurt as she? Had he gone to the ranch to lick his wounds or was he holed up in his condo, regretting the mess he'd made of their affair?

More than once, she punched his number into her phone, prepared to admit that she understood why he'd wanted to shield her from involvement in his protracted divorce. But she didn't make the call because she couldn't promise him that she'd be there when his divorce was final. As much as she yearned for the sweet surge of passion that connected them as lovers, the desire that tugged at her heart didn't overshadow the hurt that raged inside.

By late Sunday afternoon, Jewel was exhausted with herself. She went outside and sat by the pool, a pad of paper on her lap, pen in hand. It was time to pull herself together and make some serious decisions.

After flirting with the idea of leaving *P & P,* she had finally decided that quitting was not an option. She loved her role as Caprice Desmond. Her fans would be crushed if she deserted them and her contract with *The Proud and the Passionate* was still in force. She'd honor it, protecting her career at all costs. Instead of running away, she would drastically change her attitude and that could only happen if she made a new set of rules.

Jewel began to write. Rule one: While in front of the camera, lock down all good memories of Taye. Rule two: Keep Taye's deceitful behavior uppermost in my mind. Rule three: Take mental control of the situation and become my own director. Rule four: Pour every ounce of energy into delivering the best performance possible. Rule five: Only speak to Taye when it is absolutely necessary. Rule six: Listen to him, follow his direction and cautiously monitor my reactions to him.

Finished with her list, Jewel lifted her face to the last blush of California sunshine and let it warm her skin. Brad Fortune popped into her mind and she recalled how easily she'd performed under his direction. She'd felt liberated. Strong. Capable of giving him and her fans exactly what they wanted. What had happened to her? She'd given all of her emotions to Taye, not her craft, and by breaking the hold she'd allowed him to have over her, she would regain her confidence. She would return to the woman she had been before Taye Elliott entered her life and made her lose sight of what was most important: her career.

The lonely nights and empty days that Taye spent brooding at Double Pass left him feeling aimless and disappointed. Friday night, he numbed himself with too much tequila and fell asleep fully dressed on the sofa. All day Saturday, he roamed the land on horseback and then hiked into the mountains on foot, tiring himself to the point of exhaustion. On Sunday, a rainstorm blew in from the east, keeping him inside the house, where he paced from the den to the kitchen and back, cell phone in hand, tempted to call Jewel to beg her forgiveness. But he couldn't press her number. He had promised himself he'd leave her alone. He was the one who had trashed their relationship, so he deserved to feel the pain.

Why the hell didn't I tell her the truth day one? he silently raged, wishing he could turn back the clock and start over. Of all the risks he'd taken in his life, why hadn't he risked being up-front with her—the only woman he'd ever loved?

But do I really have to lose her? Taye asked himself, sucking in calming breaths to keep from tearing up. He couldn't break down again. He'd cried all he planned to over this disaster. Now, he had to clear his head and come up with a way to set things straight.

Still reeling from their argument, he had too much time on his hands: time to relive, in vivid detail, the expression on her face the last time he looked at her. The tears in her eyes, the quiver of her lips, the deep disappointment in the set of her jaw. She'd been stung by his betrayal, but he had to believe that she still loved him because he loved her and he was going to get her back.

Taye jammed his cell phone into a desk drawer and went to stand at the double-glass doors facing the rain-slicked patio. A fine white mist shrouded the mountains in the distance, just like the foggy blanket of worry that filled Taye's mind. Staring off across the land, he recalled Jewel's remark about Rona's restaurant: that it had been so busy she'd waited an hour for her food. That a regular customer said it was always packed. When he'd driven by the place a few weeks ago, cars had lined both sides of the street. She must be making money, but Vince Torini's remark about Rona's tax returns echoed in Taye's head. According to her records, Simply Delicious was still in the red.

But maybe it isn't, Taye suddenly thought, growing very still. What if she lied on her tax return? Rubbing his chin, Taye thought back to a conversation he'd had with an actor friend of his who had hired a forensic accountant to find hidden assets during his divorce. The guy's wife had owned a bar that sold imported beer. She'd claimed the bar was failing, but drove an expensive car, took fancy vacations and bought significant amounts of real estate. The forensic accountant had been able to prove that her reported sales for tax purposes were thousands of dollars lower than the actual amount of product served and in the end, the court had ruled against her in their property settlement petition.

"I've gotta get Vince to dig deeper," Taye told himself as he grabbed his cell phone out of the drawer and scrolled down to his attorney's home number.

Chapter 27

Back on the set Monday morning, Jewel stuck to her rules. She made it through her scenes with only one take each time. While involved in romantic poses with Sonny, she strengthened her resolve and refused to mentally conjure up images of Taye with his arms around her, his hot erection pressed into her thigh, his lips sliding over hers. While arguing with Janie Olsen in an explosive scene, she imagined that she was giving Taye a piece of her mind, letting him know that she refused to be his undercover woman while he worked out the kinks in his divorce.

For the remainder of the week, she avoided any personal interaction with Taye and worked hard to infuse Caprice Desmond with a more dramatic persona—making her spunkier, sexier, angrier, pushier, stronger and more demanding than ever. Immersed in her role, Jewel pulsed with energy, driving her and the rest of the cast to pull off the most powerful performances of the season.

After a long day of filming on Thursday, Fred Warner, who had been on the set all week, came to Jewel's dressing room to congratulate her on her energetic portrayal of Caprice Desmond.

"The Jewel Blaine I know and love is back on track," he gushed, sitting on the arm of the blue-and-white love seat, hands crossed on one knee. He moved his chin up and down in satisfaction while beaming his approval. "Jewel, the dailies are fantastic. The studio is really pleased with this week's episodes."

"Thanks, Fred. I appreciate your telling me that. I don't often get feedback from the suits upstairs." She laughed lightly.

"I know and I plan to tell everyone thanks for working so hard," Fred said.

"Things were a bit rocky at first, after Brad's death and all," Jewel started. "But now, I think we've all found our groove with Taye…who's really a great director." As the words spilled out, Jewel felt a catch in her throat. Taye might know his stuff when it came to directing, but he sure as hell didn't know much about women. His first marriage had been to a woman who was obviously jerking him around for money and he'd let Jewel blindside him at his own game.

"Taye's good. I can't agree more," Fred replied, placing an index finger to his lips as he studied Jewel in silence. "There's another reason I dropped by. Something I want you to be the first to know, outside of Taye, that is."

"Oh? What?" Jewel asked.

"CBC is considering a spin-off of *P & P,* with Taye Elliott directing."

Jewel put down the comb she'd been running through her hair and stared at Fred in amazement. "A spin-off?"

"That's right. We want him to be a permanent fixture here at CBC and the best way to do that is to shift right into another daytime drama that will bring *P & P*'s audience along."

"What does that mean for *P & P?* Any major changes I should know about?" Jewel probed, suddenly feeling vulnerable.

"No decisions yet. Of course we want to analyze the results of May sweeps, then we'll have a better feel for where we want to go. But don't worry, I'm all for Caprice Desmond and Darin Saintclare staying put in Elm Valley."

"Hmm, that's good, I guess," Jewel tried to joke, her stomach beginning to tighten. "When would all of these changes happen?"

"Soon. Once the numbers come in. That'll determine how the studio moves forward."

Jewel tried to act as nonplussed as possible, but her insides were quivering like crazy. Sensing Fred had revealed all he planned to, she managed to say, "Taye must be terribly excited about this."

Fred nodded. "He is. He's about to become a very bankable director with a future in daytime drama. But first, he's gotta prove his worth by pushing up *P & P's* numbers. We want him to leave the show on a high note, of course." Fred stood, preparing to leave. "Next week is gonna be the real test. I'm expecting big things from Taye as well as you, Jewel. Let's end this sweeps with a blowout, okay?" He laughed, clasped both hands to Jewel's one and then left, shutting her door with a sharp click.

Alone, Jewel thought about this turn of events, stunned that Taye was in line to get his own show, although relieved that he hadn't been tapped as the permanent director of *P & P.* So what if he became a regular fixture at the studio? It wouldn't bother her, as long as he kept his distance. In fact, this development might be the perfect solution to her dilemma.

However, Jewel's positive spin on Fred Warner's news began to lose its shine when she thought about Taye directing a new leading lady. His keen director's eyes would be trained on some sexy, new actress, not Jewel Blaine. He would step onto the set to demonstrate romantic embraces and lovemaking positions with someone else, not her. By the time his show went into production, his divorce would be final, making him one of the most eligible bachelors in Hollywood. What if he fell for someone else while on the rebound? What if she lost the only man she'd ever loved because she preferred to play by the rules instead of taking a chance on him? Could she stand by and watch while he romanced another woman? What would *that* do to her concentration?

Feelings of jealousy and insecurity began to creep in despite Jewel's efforts to keep them at bay. Frustrated, she left her dressing room and exited the building. Just as she was about to get into her car, Taye called her name from across the parking lot and hurried over.

"Wait up! Please," he called out, coming closer. "Just wanted to tell you some good news."

Jewel shrugged and pushed her sunglasses higher on her nose, deciding to be civil. Watching him walk toward her— his long legs extended, slim hips rocking from side to side, his wide shoulders so strong and muscle-bound. She swallowed a surge of longing, while her eyes swept down to his crotch, initiating images that were permanently seared in her brain. His swollen erection poised to claim her. His bulging biceps, eager to embrace. The dark intensity that came to his eyes when he lowered his mouth to hers. God, how she missed the way his hands moved over her body, leaving a trail of red-hot fire as he playfully sexed her and entertained her at the same time! Right then, she wanted nothing more than to slide down onto his hard erection and feel him pulsing inside her.

"Give me strength," she whispered to herself, growing soft and moist while her nipples grew as hard as the twin diamonds in her ears. Blinking away her erotic visions, she leaned against her car, lips parted as he stopped in front of her and grinned, initiating a fresh wave of shudders through Jewel.

"Really great news," Taye started.

"I already heard," she flipped back, trying to sound cool. "Fred told me all about your spin-off deal. Congratulations and good luck."

"Thanks. That means a lot, coming from you." His voice was low, his tone grateful.

"Well, you deserve it, Taye. Really," Jewel replied, hoping she sounded sincere because she did mean what she said, even though her heart was crowded with uncertainty about her feelings for him. "And I do understand how important next week is. I want you to know that I'll do whatever I can to get the ratings Fred wants, so you can leave *P & P* on a very high note."

Taye sighed, sounding relieved. "Thanks, Jewel. I was hoping you'd feel that way." He stepped closer. "Along those lines…think we could get together tomorrow and hash out a few rough spots in the script? I know Friday is the day you like to set aside to work on your lines by yourself, but what about it?"

Jewel frowned and shook her head. "No. Not a good idea, Taye. Don't press me, okay?"

"I'm not. Only for work, I promise, Jewel," Taye pleaded in earnest. "I really want to go over that dream sequence you have to do. It's the finale of the story line and it's gotta come off right."

Stiffening her spine, Jewel locked cool eyes with Taye, deciding it was time to test this man and see what he was made of. Or did she want to test herself? "Fine. You're the director, so if you're calling for a rehearsal, I can't refuse, can I?"

"Sure you can, but I don't want you to." Taye put a hand on the side of her car and leaned in, capturing her within a suffocating space. Jewel tensed, but didn't pull away as his lemony scent spiraled into her brain. "I miss you, Jewel," Taye whispered. "I was wrong to keep quiet about the divorce. I deserve the cold shoulder and more. But don't build a wall between us now. Not when next week is so important for both of us. You're doing fantastic work and I can see now that I'd been hindering your talent. I'm sorry. But where we need to go with this story line now is over the top. Do you trust me to make that happen?"

Jewel inclined her head, unable to speak.

"Good. With your talent and my direction, if we work together we can create the kind of magic that'll drive fans wild."

The silence between them zinged with anticipation. Jewel let the tension in her shoulders slip away, lifting her face to Taye. They shared a creative mission that transcended their faltering personal connection and she wasn't about to back away from his taunting offer to rehearse together.

"Think we can bring in the highest ratings in *P & P* history?" he enthusiastically challenged.

"Yes! Of course we can," Jewel stated with pride. "I have no problem working with you, as long as we both remember where we stand. How this story line wraps is more important than you or me."

"Absolutely! Oh God, thanks, Jewel. Strictly business, I promise."

"It had better be. All right. What time do you want to get together? Your office or on the set?"

"That's the twist…I've gotta be at the ranch all day Friday. Whit's away for the week and the real estate agent wants to meet me there to discuss some details about the property. Can you meet me there tomorrow? About noon?"

Jewel froze. How dare he ask that of her after all they'd been through? What kind of a joke was this? He must think she was nuts! "The ranch?"

"Yes. It'll be quiet. The best place to work."

I'll bet, Jewel thought, tucking her bottom lip beneath her teeth, considering what to do. Taye was testing her, challenging her to be alone with him at the place where they'd shared their most intimate moments. Well, fine. She'd play his game and win. Why refuse? They did need to go over next week's scenes to guarantee through-the-roof ratings and she planned to deliver. Jewel mentally ran through her list of rules, pushed aside her emotional fears and pulled on her newfound sense of strength. Now was not the time to show a hint of weakness.

"No problem," she told Taye, ready to show him how quickly she'd recovered. "See you there at about noon." She opened her car door and started to get in, but turned back to tell Taye, "Don't send a car. I know my way to Double Pass and I can drive myself." *And I'll stick to my rules, not let you touch me and leave before it gets dark.*

Chapter 28

The smell of grilled lobster, spiced shrimp and garlic aspara-
gus lingered in the room long after Taye had cleared away the
dirty dishes. The wonderful scents mingled sweetly with the
fragrance of the oversize bouquet of white roses that sat in the
center of the low coffee table, where a silver ice bucket held a
bottle of champagne.

Taye leaned over, removed the bottle, filled two glasses and
handed one to Jewel.

"So, I have to give you credit for putting me on that path,"
he told her. "As strange as it sounds, your going to Rona's restaurant was the best thing that could have ever happened."

"So, you're saying that Rona has been lying about her
business? She lied on her tax returns?" Jewel remarked, taking
a sip of her drink and then scooting to the far end of the leather
couch to better see Taye and increase the space between them.

So far, Taye had kept his promise and they'd focused on the
work, spending the entire afternoon running lines, discussing
motivation, dissecting story line and plotting strategy for next

week's episodes. They'd been so engrossed in *P & P* that they hadn't stopped working until after eight o'clock, when Taye insisted that Jewel stay for dinner, which he offered to cook.

Now, a bottle of champagne seemed to be dashing Jewel's plans to get in her car and head home before dark.

"That's right," Taye continued. "My attorney called me with the news this morning. The forensic accountant he put on the case was able to get proof that Rona's restaurant is doing very well. Seems her seafood and wholesale rice orders tripped the alarm. She's selling a lot more food than reported and has a lot to explain."

Jewel watched Taye closely. He seemed nervous, emotionally drained and tense. She wanted to clasp her arms around him, let him rest his head on her shoulder and tell him that she understood what he'd been going through. He'd been deliberately lied to, used and disrespected by his estranged wife. He'd been humiliated, just as Chandler Jeffries had humiliated her. "So, you don't have to sell Double Pass?"

"Nope. I met with the real estate agent and we took it off the market this morning."

"And your divorce?" she had to ask.

"Got a court date for Monday. With the ammunition from the forensic accountant, Vince got Rona to drop her challenge to the property settlement. I'll be a free man by Monday afternoon."

The look Taye gave Jewel made her freeze. It was intense, level and much too serious. What did he want her to say? That all was forgiven? Congratulations on your impending freedom? Let's hop back into bed and celebrate? No, she wasn't about to go there. Not yet, at least. "To the end of the shoot," she toasted, stalling for time to sort out her reaction to his news.

"To the end of the shoot," Taye agreed, and then added, "And to the beginning of…?" He paused, one eyebrow raised, waiting for Jewel to finish his sentence.

Without missing a beat, she took up the challenge, "To the beginning of whatever is meant to come next," she stated, placing her glass to her lips.

"I'll drink to that," Taye agreed, his eyes lingering on her as he drank.

The stretch of silence that followed their toast was filled by soft jazz music coming from the CD player, blended with night sounds from the desert that wafted in through open patio doors. The mood was comfortable, familiar and much too memorable for Jewel, who wanted nothing more than to sink into Taye's arms and drown in his kisses.

"What're you thinking?" Taye interrupted, easing closer to Jewel.

Startled back to the moment, Jewel zeroed in on the emotional roller coaster that had been rushing through her all afternoon. "Thinking about our toast…to whatever is meant to come next. I wonder what that will be."

"Me, too." Taye studied her with a gaze as soft as a caress. "How do you feel right now?" he ventured.

"I feel at loose ends," Jewel replied. "Unsure. Not because of what's happened with us…but because this story line is ending," she murmured, not objecting when he shifted close enough to touch his knee to hers. She laughed under her breath. "I get like this sometimes. Saying goodbye to a story line is hard." Another low chuckle. "Sound crazy?"

"Not at all. I've been there. When a movie is over and the cast members move on, it's difficult to get back to the regular world. Separating from the fantasy world you've worked so hard to create to reenter the real world, can be jolting. Even a little depressing."

"Yeah," Jewel whispered, relieved that he understood what she was trying to say. "And then a new story line starts up and everyone gets excited. It's as if the old one never existed. But in soap land, the past is never completely forgotten, we just move on, adding new layers to our story."

"And that's how it could happen with us, Jewel," Taye said, raking her with intense eyes. "Our story line doesn't have to end. We can turn the page on the script, add more scenes, learn from the past and make the future story even better."

"I don't know about that," Jewel offered in a tentative voice.

"Well, I refuse to let it end like this. Please, Jewel. Stick with me. Think about the life we can create once my divorce is final. I'm leaving *P & P* anyway, so you won't have to worry about any conflict on the set. We can be out in the open with our love. Act like a normal couple." He paused. "But I am gonna miss telling Caprice Desmond what to do. You're just like Caprice, you know?" he joked.

Jewel rocked back, jerking her neck. "Why'd you say that?" she asked suspiciously.

"Caprice is a woman who knows what she wants and makes sure she gets it. You do, too. And I love you for that." He lazily appraised her, taunting her to react.

Jewel narrowed her eyes, as if trying to see him more clearly. He was wearing was a pair of lightweight khaki slacks and a tight navy silk T-shirt that defined his bulging biceps and enhanced six-pack abs, making her suddenly grow hot all over. "You're making this very hard," she said, her resistance beginning to melt.

"I'm just glad you agreed to come out to the ranch."

"We accomplished a lot, didn't we?" Jewel said in a flurry of words that tumbled out and made Taye's eyes light up.

"More than I'd expected," he agreed.

"I hadn't planned on staying so late."

"I hate to think of you driving home alone."

"I'll be all right," she replied, though not looking forward to the dark, lonely drive.

"Stay." Taye said the word with tenderness.

"I can't," Jewel sharply snapped.

"Yes, you could," Taye countered in a much stronger tone. "I want to be with you…not for one night in the country. Forever. As your partner in life."

Although his words aroused old fears and uncertainties, she could feel her anger beginning to smooth out, like honey melting in the sun. She wanted him for more than one night, too. She was exhausted with pretending she didn't care. Why turn her back on love when she could shake off the past and claim her man?

With a crack, Jewel set down her empty champagne glass and reached for Taye, deciding, rules be damned! She gripped his shoulders with both hands and slipped lower on the sofa, bringing Taye along with her. "Right now, this is all I want."

She held on tight as he worked her jeans and her panties down until they lay on the floor. Eyes closed, she felt him undressing, felt his fingers press into her, felt her body go wet and slick. Without ending their connection, she raked his back with tender fingers, massaging his rock-hard buttocks.

"Taye, you're making me crazy," she groaned against his chest.

"But crazy like a woman in love, I hope."

And that was all she needed to hear because he had spoken the truth. Everything had changed. Their relationship had a chance. He wasn't just a married man who'd expected her to go along with his shaky program. He'd taken action to free himself and she loved him all the more for that.

A breeze that smelled of cactus flowers and mountain air swelled into the room. Jewel drew in the heady essence of the countryside, wanting to capture the scent to store away and draw on when she and Taye were apart.

When he drove his swollen erection into her, teasing her hips into a rocking, pounding dance of pulse and heat, Jewel gasped in delight. How lucky was she to have found love so accidentally? For it to have bloomed so quickly and intensely? Changing her life in a heartbeat.

The pace of their reunion came at Jewel with dizzying speed. She placed the palms of her hands against Taye's chest and braced herself, eager to follow his direction.

Chapter 29

The heat on the set of *The Proud and the Passionate* steadily rose as Jewel put herself in Taye's expert hands. Vibrating with energy and flush with confidence, she drew on the sizzling sex they'd shared at Double Pass to inspire her riveting performances. No longer guilty, confused or torn about her love for Taye, she felt unencumbered and free to expose her innermost emotions. When she was not before the cameras she was making plans for a future with Taye, or going shopping with Marlena, or lunching with industry friends. Her newfound sense of romantic security rejuvenated Jewel, erasing the nagging doubts she'd had about herself and Taye.

After sweeps week ended, she would have a four-week hiatus, which she planned to spend relaxing at Double Pass with Taye, soaking up the mountain air. For the first time in her life, she understood the inner peace that came from being loved and from allowing herself to love in return.

When the ratings came in, it was clear that Caprice Desmond's new raw sexuality had pleased the studio, the advertisers and the faithful fans of *P & P.* The explosive cliff-hanger finale was a smash. E-mails filled with accolades flooded in. Ratings looked good. Fred Warner was very happy.

Chapter 30

"A soap opera's destiny isn't measured only by ratings points and share," Fred Warner stated, rocking back in his black leather executive chair to study Taye with calculating eyes. "We use feedback from viewers, fan letters, market research and input from advertisers as well as the weekly Nielsen ratings."

"I know how it works," Taye interjected, anxious for Fred to get on with whatever he'd called him into his office to say. "The network has to consider a variety of factors that impact the success or failure of a show."

Fred nodded. "Our profitability depends first of all on revenue from advertisers and sponsors, and those rates are influenced not only by the total number of viewers, but also by particular demographics, such as age, sex and economic class."

Taye let the producer's words hang between them, sensing that Fred really didn't want or need to hear anything from Taye.

"A daytime drama must have an exciting story line, that's true. But the characters also have to give the viewers smaller moments that resonate with them, connect with their lives and pull them deeper into the story." Fred tilted his upper body forward, pressing against the edge of his desk, braced by his white-sleeved forearms. "Unfortunately, Taye, that's been missing from *The Proud and the Passionate* all season and it's the reason why ratings tanked."

"But I don't understand," Taye started. "We came up a full point and I think the final week brought home a winner. Isn't that proof that things are starting to gel?"

Fred shrugged while toying with a slim silver pen, his eyes downcast. "The studio has made its decision about the spin-off we discussed last week."

"And?" Taye prompted, beginning to feel uneasy.

Fred raised his gaze, cocked a brow and gave Taye a crooked half smile. "It's been green-lighted. Lori Callyer will be head writer and Sonny Burton lead actor. It'll be the first daytime drama with an African-American director and a black male as the central figure. I think it's gonna be huge."

Taye eased back in his chair, taking in Fred's announcement, thrilled with the news, yet concerned. If Sonny was cast as the lead character, where did that leave Jewel? "This is great, Fred. We got a working title?"

"Reach for Tomorrow."

"Love it," Taye remarked, unable to stop smiling.

"Here's what we want, Taye. Reality, relevance, raciness. You and Sonny give us that and you'll be on track for a successful show."

Taye ran a hand across his chin, relieved to know that his future at CBC was solid, but his head still buzzed with questions. A slow curl of apprehension wound its way into Taye's gut, giving him pause. Something wasn't right. "Who's gonna replace Sonny Burton as Darin Saintclare on *P & P?*" Taye asked, easing the conversation back to the show he'd just moved up one point in the ratings war.

Fred carefully placed his silver pen back into its holder, taking his time before replying. "No one. CBC has decided to cancel *P & P. Reach* will take over that time slot." A short pause before he went on. "Taye, you really brought the ratings up on *P & P* and proved your talent, but the show's been sliding downhill all year. Your blowout finale was great, but it didn't convince the guys upstairs that *P & P* deserves another season. For now, we're gonna fill the time slot with reruns of *Proud* starting with the first episode, so new fans can get to know Darin Saintclare. We'll splice in teaser clips of *Reach,* and then launch the new show in September. The executives want to devote all of their resources to the spin-off instead of splitting the audience between two shows."

"But Jewel? Where is she going?" Taye was frantic. "Does she even know about this?" His voice resonated with shock.

"No, and for now, don't say anything. This is just a heads-up for you. There're a lot of details still in play. I plan to talk to Jewel as soon as we finalize the buyout terms of her contract, so keep this to yourself, okay?"

Taye could only stare at Fred in amazement. Jewel was being let go? He was getting his own show? How in hell would she ever get over this? *P & P* was her life. She *was* Caprice Desmond. A blow like this was really going to hit Jewel hard and Taye wanted to be there for her, convince her that he had had no idea this would happen. But why would she want him around while she cried her eyes out and he made plans to take over her time slot? Oh, hell. This was totally ridiculous.

"As you know," Fred was saying, "Jewel Blaine is a very good actress. She'll easily land on another soap. These things happen. Jewel knows the score…in this business, nothing is ever guaranteed. It's not personal, this is strictly business."

But you aren't the one who will have to convince her, Taye thought, dreading what was about to happen.

Chapter 31

When the "You've Got Mail" alert popped up at the bottom of her computer screen, Jewel glanced at it, decided it could wait and continued processing her online purchase of three novels she planned to take to Double Pass and read during her hiatus. She had given Carmie a two-week vacation and with the season finale wrapped and the best work she'd done in years out there on the screen for her fans, she couldn't be happier.

Earlier, Jewel had spoken with Suzy Rabu when she'd called Taye to discuss their dinner plans and his assistant had revealed the good news: *P & P* had moved up a full point in the ratings and Fred was over the moon about that.

"I knew we'd pull it off," Jewel said to herself, beaming in satisfaction at the computer screen. "All because of Taye. He's made me a better actress and I owe him a lot." After clicking the Pay button and finalizing her book purchase, she surfed over to the Beautiful Brides Web site to check out the dresses, veils and wedding tips, something she had begun to do on a regular basis as she planned her future with Taye.

His divorce was final. He was free. They were madly in love and rarely apart, spending weeknights at her house and weekends at Double Pass. He hadn't actually proposed yet, but Jewel wasn't worried. After such a stressful contest with his ex-wife, Taye deserved space to regroup before launching into a second marriage. However, Jewel was content to use this time to dream up the perfect wedding.

When a second e-mail alert popped up, Jewel clicked the icon to see what had come into the private e-mail address that she reserved for studio business. Although officially on hiatus, she knew well enough that the inner workings of a daytime drama never took a vacation.

Accessing her mail, she opened a message from Taye suggesting they meet at Bon Ami for dinner. She smiled, recalling her first meeting with Taye at the restaurant and how intrigued she'd been with him.

Funny how life works out, she mused. Because her mind had been on Taye when she left Bon Ami, she'd hit that van. Because of the accident, she'd gone to see Ruth Hardwick and overheard two strangers talking about Rona Elliott, from whom she'd uncovered the truth about Taye's marriage. And the lawyer's area of expertise had also inspired a challenge to help Taye uncover the truth about his ex-wife's business.

Jewel sat quietly, thinking about all that had happened and how easily one unexpected event cascades into another, initiating forces that can change a person's life.

With a sigh of contentment, she clicked on the second e-mail, which was from Fred Warner. *I hope he's not asking me to shorten my vacation,* Jewel thought as she opened the message and began to read. However, as soon as she read the first line, she gasped. Something was wrong with this message. The salutation was to Art Freeman, not to her. So, why had she been copied? Curious, she began to read.

Art: I met with Taye. Told him the spin-off has been green-lighted for fall schedule and that P & P has been cancelled. When will Jewel's buyout package be firm? I'd like to meet with her before any of this leaks. Get back to me asap. Fred

A plume of fear plunged through Jewel, searing her nerves, making her body zing with shock. She covered her mouth with both hands and read the message two more times. Clearly, it had not been meant for her. She'd gotten it by mistake and wasn't supposed to know. Not yet. But Taye knew. And he hadn't told her.

How in hell did this happen? What exactly did Fred mean and why wasn't she warned about this? Jewel's outrage rose like a plume of fire, burning its way to the surface. Even though *P & P*'s ratings had improved, she was out of a job and Taye was moving on to a new show? How unfair was that?

He'd known what he was doing when he romanced her at the ranch. She had been naive to let him make love to her, get her to trust him enough to help him bring up the ratings. That's all he'd wanted, to secure his shot at a spin-off.

"Well, Fred Warner has some explaining to do and I want to hear what he has to say," she decided, grabbing the phone.

Her first words to Fred Warner were, "What the hell is going on? And you'd better be up-front with me!"

Fred, horrified to learn that his e-mail had been misdirected, told Jewel, "Yes. As difficult as it is for me to tell you this, *P & P* is slated for cancellation. Sonny Burton is moving to *Reach for Tomorrow,* Taye Elliott's spin-off, and there just doesn't seem to be a future for the character of Caprice Desmond, so we've decided not to green-light another season for *P & P.* But don't worry, you'll be well-compensated for the remainder of your contract."

Stunned by Fred's cold, calculating response, Jewel lashed out. "I thought I knew you, Fred. I thought you were looking out for my best interests, but apparently you've been looking out for Mr. Elliott's instead. What a shabby way to treat our professional relationship."

"It's not personal, Jewel. And it wasn't up to me. I fought cancellation, but I was outvoted."

"Right! As if you really cared. And as for my compensation, I'll have my attorney call you because I am not going to let this go without a fight."

"Understood," Fred relented. "I'm sure your attorney and CBC can come to an acceptable agreement. Good luck, Jewel. I mean that. You deserve it." Then the line went dead.

Jewel gasped, stared at the silent phone for a split second and then punched in Taye's number, her fingers trembling as they flew over the keypad, her mind set to give him hell.

"Hey, you got my e-mail?" Taye said as soon as he came on the line. "Wanna meet for drinks at Sugar's before we go to dinner at Bon Ami? I've got so much to tell you. This has been one crazy day!"

"Screw you, Taye!" Jewel shouted. "No, I don't want to have a drink, or dinner, or anything with you. Not tonight, not ever again! I'll just bet you've got a ton of news to tell me. Let me guess. The name of your new show, perhaps? Oh, let me think…could it be *Reach for Tomorrow?* And I wonder who the new lead actor is? Could it be Sonny Burton, my faithful costar? So, who doesn't have a job right now? Oh! Me! *I don't* have a job at CBC anymore. Right?"

"Who told you?" Taye asked warily.

"Not you! So what the hell what does it matter?"

"Jewel, believe me, I knew nothing about the executive's decision to cancel *P & P.* Fred sprang the news on me this afternoon and I was as shocked as you are."

"I doubt that!"

"Okay, I agree, it's not fair. It's ugly and hurtful and shocking. You don't deserve this…but it's business, Jewel. You've been involved in television long enough to know shit happens. And when it does, you've gotta move on."

"Shut up! What do you know about television, let alone daytime drama? You've been in it how long? Two months? You are one sorry brother, you know that? You romanced me simply to get a better performance outta me and I can't think of a lower, dirtier thing to do to someone you're supposed to care about."

"Absolutely not true. I love you. No way would I deliberately use you or hurt you."

"You knew all along that Sonny was going over to the lead role in your show and that the set of *P & P* was about to go dark."

"No, I didn't. But we both were aware that *P & P* was not doing as well as the studio wanted. Its future was in question. Right?"

Jewel refused to answer, so Taye continued to press his case. "The studio simply made a decision to cut their losses and try something new. It was their call and there was nothing I could have done to make them change their minds."

"Hmm! You know what? I can guarantee *Reach* won't succeed, Taye. Not unless you put your tired player's moves on your new lead actress and fool her into sleeping with you. What a joke! But I'm not laughing. I'm through. Goodbye, Taye. Sorry I can't wish you good luck."

Taye cupped his hands and sank his head into his palms, emotionally shredded by what was happening. He should have been prepared for the hollow pain that engulfed him, but he'd been so focused on his good news that he hadn't processed just how hard this would be on Jewel. She'd hit back like a tiger protecting a cub, crushed by the collapse of a career that had meant everything to her.

Taye grabbed his car keys and slammed out of his office, desperate to get away from the studio. He had no dinner plans now, no place he had to be, but he sure as hell didn't want any of his colleagues to catch him with tears brimming in his eyes when he ought to be celebrating his new show. Suddenly the spin-off deal didn't seem so wonderful. He was moving forward in his career, but failing at love. Things were not turning out as he had planned.

Shaking with frustration, Jewel chastised herself. She had no one to blame for her trouble but herself. She had allowed a romantic involvement with her director to distract her when she should have been paying attention to her career. *It's not the end of the world,* she decided, grasping for emotional control. Down for Love *wants me as a lead contract player. I can be back on the air before* Reach for Tomorrow *even gets into production. I'll show CBC and Taye Elliott what kind of power I have.*

After taking time to drink a cup of tea and compose herself, Jewel called Marlena Kirk.

"Damn, that's bad news," Marlena said after hearing Jewel explain what had happened.

"Yeah, really. I never dreamed CBC would treat me like this."

"Well, you'll probably walk away with enough cash to take a much-needed vacation. Relax, pull yourself together and then we'll talk. I'll get you back to work."

"That's why I called, Marlena. I want that role at *Down for Love.* I can start right away. Who needs a vacation? I want to get right back on the air. Call the casting director at *DFL* and set up a meeting, okay?"

"Gee, Jewel. I wish I could, but that part's already been cast. Some starlet from Italy got it. Maria Monetti. Cute, but not in a dramatic way. Not like you."

"What? I thought they wanted me!"

"At first, yes, but when I got back to the producer to tell him you weren't interested, he said the dramatic slippage of *The Proud and the Passionate*'s ratings early in the sweeps was working against you. They were no longer interested and were going with someone else." A tense silence followed.

"You never told me that! I assumed the offer still stood." Jewel was trembling with anger, sick to her stomach, terrified about her future.

"There're a lot of things I don't tell you…and be glad I don't," Marlena said. "Stop worrying about another contract. I'll start making calls right away and I promise to find a better role than *DFL* or *P & P.* Leave it to me. I'll get back to you in a few days."

When Jewel clicked Off, she felt weak. Her world had collapsed! In the space of an hour, she had fallen from acclaimed actress on a daytime drama to the biggest joke in the industry. The trades were going to run stories about *P & P*'s cancellation and the spin-off set to launch without her in the fall. Photos of hot and hunky Taye Elliott, along with the story of how he went from stuntman to director, would be featured, while the only mention of Jewel Blaine would be the fact that she was unemployed! How the hell had she let this happen?

Chapter 32

Marlena fingered her heavy gold loop earring while mentally replaying her conversation with Jewel. What a bummer! Knowing Jewel as she did, Marlena was certain her friend was about to have a breakdown over this setback in her career.

"Damn, I should have pursued the deal at *DFL*," Marlena muttered, feeling as if she'd let her client down. *Well, there's nothing to do when you're knocked down but get back up and start fighting,* Marlena decided, scrolling through her contact list to plot her pitch to reignite Jewel's career.

After an hour of phone calls and callbacks, Marlena was impressed with the number of possible roles she'd found for Jewel. *Why in the world does CBC want to let Jewel Blaine go? Why cancel a show as popular as* The Proud and the Passionate *based on ratings that are good but not great? The studio is making a terrible mistake. I wonder how Caprice Desmond would react to being told she was no longer wanted?* Marlena mused as she logged on to *P & P*'s Web site to surf around and see what was going on.

She wasn't surprised to see that news of the demise of *The Proud and the Passionate* was already circulating on the Web. However, she was surprised to see that a number of bloggers had posted petitions for fans to protest the cancellation of their favorite show.

"Good move," Marlena said, deciding to join in the effort. With the click of her mouse, she launched a massive e-mail blast to all of her industry contacts, asking them to support the return of *P & P.*

Chapter 33

For the next three days, Jewel took no phone calls, answered no e-mails and did not leave her house. She deleted Taye's text messages and voice mails without reading or listening to them. Marlena's inquiries about Jewel's mental state went unanswered, too. All Jewel wanted to hear from Marlena was news about a juicy new role that would put her where she belonged—back in a soap opera, in front of fans who loved and appreciated her.

By the fourth day of her self-imposed confinement, Jewel was beginning to feel like an animal in a cage, so she pulled on a pair of jeans, a baggy shirt, her standard floppy hat and over-size sunglasses to make a quick run to Royal Street Market and stock up on enough mango sherbet to get her through this distressing time.

What first caught her eye when she entered the grocery store were the headlines and photos splashed across the covers of *Soap Opera Gossip* magazine. P & P *Dumps Caprice, but Darin Moves On. Jewel Blaine in Hiding /Sonny Burton Set to Emerge on New Show. The Inside Scoop on the Hottest New Daytime Director! Who Is Taye Elliott and Where Did He Come From?*

Jewel's stomach heaved in disgust to see what her career had come down to. A few titillating headlines on gossip rags for grocery shoppers to read. Head bent, she went to the frozen-food aisle, grabbed two buckets of the frozen dessert and moved quickly into the Express Pay line. Thank God, no one recognized her. The last thing she wanted was for some stranger to push a piece of paper in her face and ask her for an autograph.

Taye locked his car door and started across the Royal Street Market parking lot, mentally reciting the list of things he needed to buy. AA batteries for his TV remote, shaving cream and enough frozen dinners to get him through the weekend. With work already under way on *Reach,* he was staying in his condo in Marina del Rey and had no time or interest in cooking. He had scripts to read, scenes to block and meetings with studio execs, set directors, costume directors and others responsible for the success of his show.

He was feeling good about the way it was coming together and the long hours kept his mind off personal matters, for a short while at least. He missed Jewel like crazy, felt horrible about the way things had turned out for her, but knew she needed time and space to process what had happened. But how much time and how much space? That, he didn't know.

The automatic doors swung open. Taye walked in, eyes darting around the store to find the aisle he wanted. As he passed the checkout counter, a lady's hat caught his attention. He stopped in midstride and lifted his sunglasses, wanting to be certain before he spoke. "Jewel!" She was wearing the sun hat and glasses she'd worn on their first date. When they'd gone to The Grove. When he'd fallen in love. When he'd realized he did not want to live without her. He hurried over just as she grabbed her plastic bag of groceries and headed toward the exit.

"Hello, Taye," she replied in a flat voice, not breaking her stride as she exited through the automatic door.

Taye increased his pace, followed her outside, talking as fast as he could. "Hey. Can we talk for a minute? Don't run off. Stop. Please!"

She swung around and glared at him. "I have nothing to say to you."

"Well, I have something to say to you. I miss you, Jewel. Didn't you get my messages? Where have you been? I've been worried about you."

"I've been at home and I am fine," she muttered, walking away, even faster.

"Can we get together? Talk this out? Please? You gotta know how I feel about this."

"Sorry, I don't know anything about that." She pressed the remote to her car and when it beeped, she reached for the door handle.

Taye moved forward, quickly covering her hand with his. "No. Don't go. Not yet."

She studied him for a moment and then snatched her hand from his. "You've got a lot of nerve, you know? Why the hell should I talk to you?"

He grabbed the opening to press his case. "Because we have unfinished business."

"I don't think so."

"Can we sit in your car? For five minutes? Please. I just want to say something to you."

Without answering, Jewel slid in behind the wheel and when she didn't start the engine, Taye rushed over to the passenger door, opened it and got in.

"Jewel, you've gotta listen to me."

"I don't have to do *anything!* Stop bossing me around. You are no longer my director, understand?"

"I didn't mean it like that."

"Yeah. Right. Do you ever mean anything you say?"

"I meant it when I said I love you. I did and still do. Don't let this situation with CBC break us up. Neither you nor I had any control over what the studio decided to do. If I had known they were going to cancel *P & P,* I would have fought hard against it."

"You knew how much was riding on the sweeps, that cancellation was a possibility. That's the only reason you pumped up the romantic moves. To secure your future with the studio, at the expense of mine."

"So not true. Everyone involved in the show knew we had a lot to prove in the final week. We pulled it off, but it was too late." He threw up his hands in frustration and closed his eyes for a moment, attempting to calm down. "Oh, what the hell. If you don't want to believe me, then don't."

"I wish I could, but you've made it awfully difficult."

"Jewel. Can't we put all of that aside and focus on us? I don't want to lose you. I want to marry you. Please don't blame me because my career is taking off and yours is going through a temporary redirection. That's all it is, you know? A temporary detour. Probably to something bigger and better than *P & P.* You have so much talent…this cancellation might be a blessing in disguise. Ever think that maybe it is time for you to leave daytime? Go after a role in a major motion picture?"

Jewel flashed a cutting glare at Taye. "That shows how little you know about me. I love daytime TV," she replied, anger laced in her words. "All I ever wanted to be was a television actress and my dream came true when I became Caprice Desmond. This is *my* life, Taye. Worry about your own career and let me worry about mine."

Taye tilted back his head and stared through the windshield, processing what she'd just said. Turning to her, he spoke in a gentler voice. "Do you remember what I told you about my father and my brothers?"

Jewel watched him with eyes that were a little less filled with bitterness and disappointment. "Yes," she replied. "You said your relationship with your father wasn't very good. That your brothers always ridiculed you for going into show business instead of medicine."

"Yeah. They called me a fool for throwing away a ready-made career. Said I'd never succeed in Hollywood. But they were wrong. I'm doing just fine, and..." Taye smiled wistfully and then nodded. "You know what?"

"What?"

"I've patched things up with my dad. Guess he's decided life's too short to hold grudges. We've actually been talking on the phone every few days and enjoying it. I invited my dad, my brothers and their families to Double Pass for a reunion party this weekend and all nineteen of them are coming."

"So you can celebrate your new show, I guess?"

A beat before he answered. "Sure, but I also want to bring them into my world and let them know how much I care about them. Why not share my good fortune with my nieces and nephews and sisters-in-law? I'm tired of being alone, Jewel. I want my family around me now." He reached out and touched Jewel's arm, relieved that she didn't jerk away. "I'd like for you to be a part of it. I'd liked my family to meet you. Will you come?"

Jewel replied with a sharp huff of disdain. "Thanks, but no thanks. I'll pass."

"Why? I wish you'd forget about CBC and their stupid decision. It's done. Move on. Forget about career-related problems for one day and come get to know my family. Then you might understand what kind of a guy I really am and give me another chance to prove how much I love you."

Jewel shook her head. "Sorry, I don't think I can make it. Why would I want to get to know your family after what you've done to me? Why would I want to see you surrounded by your adoring brothers and nieces and nephews, who'll probably treat you like royalty? After all, you are a successful Hollywood director with a new show. I'm just an unemployed, ex-soap opera star. You can't be serious, Taye." Jewel stuck her key into the ignition, but didn't start the car.

Taye watched her cautiously, not wanting her to go. "If you change your mind, just come out to the ranch. You don't have

to call. My house is yours. You'll always be welcome there."
Then, Taye got out of her car, the hard slam of her car door his
only goodbye.

Did Taye think she was a pushover? That he could make her
forget the damage he'd done simply because he'd said, "I love
you"? That was not going to happen. Jewel squeezed her eyes
shut, wishing she didn't love Taye so damn much, yet fearful
of resuming their intense affair. She didn't want to lose him,
but what point was there in rehashing their problems? Problems
he had caused. He was asking too much of her and the delicate
truce she'd made with her emotions was at the breaking point.

*I've gotta be strong. Resist. If I don't leave now, I might give
in, and I sure as hell can't backslide again.* Jewel shifted,
blinked away tears and adjusted her rearview mirror to watch
Taye as he walked away. His stride was quick, definite, resolute.
Sending a signal that he was finished with her.

A sharp sob bubbled up and cut off Jewel's breath, shatter-
ing her fragile composure. Through a sheen of tears, she
watched him drive away, shaken by the fact that she'd finally
let go of the man she adored. Had she been foolish to dream of
a future with him? Naive to hope for the kind of love that would
never come from millions of faceless fans? If so, she had to
admit that her silly, rigid rules had failed and now, she had to
make a decision: create a new set of rules to follow or follow
her heart.

Chapter 34

The iron gate guarding Double Pass was flung wide and cars lined both sides of the curving gravel drive. Jewel took a deep breath, bit down on her bottom lip and pulled her Lexus into an empty space at the far end of the driveway, not wanting to get too close too soon. It had taken all of her nerve to drive to Double Pass today and she still wasn't sure she was doing the right thing.

She got out of her car and assessed the scene. Some boys and a girl were kicking a soccer ball back and forth on the grassy area in front of the house, while a scattering of adults milled around and cheered them on. Old-school rock and roll music drifted from the patio, competing with raucous laughter, high-spirited chatter and the sound of horseshoes ringing against iron stakes.

Why am I here? Jewel worried, struggling with her decision to go after the man she loved, fearing he might not want her now. She'd been so mean to him. So consumed with the cancellation of her show that she'd lost sight of what was important: her happiness with Taye and all the passion, comfort and joy that he'd brought into her life.

Jewel started across the lawn, feeling very self-conscious and out of place, but determined not to run. *This is what I have to do, if I want my man back,* she kept telling herself as she stepped onto the patio and joined the lively crowd.

"Oh my God! It's Jewel Blaine!" a woman who was sunning by the pool shouted, jumping up.

Jewel's head popped around in surprise.

The woman raced to toss her paper plate of barbecue into a trash barrel and hurried over to Jewel. "It is you, isn't it?" she gushed, eyes wide in wonder as she wiped her hands on a paper napkin and then extended one to Jewel. "I'm Sandra. Taye's sister-in-law. Married to Cliff, the family lawyer."

Turning on her megawatt, fan-friendly smile, Jewel acquiesced with a gracious, "Uh, hi. And yes. It's me…Jewel Blaine. Glad to meet you." She shook Sandra's hand and glanced around. "This is quite a gathering."

"Isn't it wonderful? Our first family reunion. And in California, too! We're all so proud of Taye. And the kids can't wait to go to Disneyland."

"I know that's right," Jewel tossed back, greeting another, younger woman in a swimsuit with a towel wrapped around her hips.

"Oh…I love Caprice Desmond. Absolutely love her…and love you…well, you know what I mean," the girl squealed.

"Thanks," Jewel replied, as others began to gather around to see what all the fuss was about. "I appreciate that comment. I loved playing Caprice."

The girl ran her fingers through wet curly hair. "I'm Brenda. Taye's niece. From Chicago. And I've gotta say…I'm royally pissed that *P & P* got cancelled. What was that about?"

Oh, boy. Here it comes, Jewel thought, not wanting to go there, regretting she'd intruded on Taye's family party, wondering where he was and what she'd say to him when she saw him.

"Yeah," another woman commented, joining the conversation. "I was shocked when I read online that Darin Saintclare is gonna stick around, but Caprice is gone. No way!" She finished her chicken leg, pushed her sunglasses higher on her nose and leaned in closer to Jewel. "What is wrong with CBC? *Proud* was my favorite soap." She swallowed a mouthful of food and went on. "Now, you know I'm gonna watch *Reach for Tomorrow,* 'cause that's Taye's show, but I don't think it was right to cancel *P & P.*"

A murmur of agreement rippled through the men and women who now encircled Jewel. She glanced around, suddenly feeling very much alone. Here she was holding court with Taye's relatives and he didn't even know she was on the property. She hadn't come to make a scene. She'd come to let him know that she was sorry for pushing him away, for blaming him for something he had not been able to control and that more than anything in the world she wanted him back in her life.

"Uh, network decisions aren't made by the actors," she was telling a man who looked like an older version of Taye. "I understand how you guys feel. I'm gonna miss Elm Valley, Darin Saintclare and Caprice, too," she joked, trying to put a light spin on the subject, while wanting desperately to sink into the ground and disappear.

"What about *Reach for Tomorrow?* Why can't you get Taye to put Caprice on that show?" a slim girl in striped capri pants asked, eyes lit with expectation.

"Let me tell you why," a melodious and familiar voice stated with authority, making Jewel gasp in surprise and spin around.

"Marlena!" Jewel anchored a fist at her hip and jerked her neck, caught totally off guard. "What're you doing here?" she demanded.

"Eating barbecue, playing horseshoes and talking to Taye about the fact that your millions of fans have saved *P & P* from cancellation." Marlena focused on the girl in the red capri pants. "You're hearing it first…. *The Proud and the Passionate* will return in the fall and Jewel Blaine will return as Caprice Desmond."

"What? Is that true?" Jewel blurted, just as Taye emerged from the house holding a tray of hamburger buns. He set the food on a poolside table and walked over to stand beside Jewel.

"Marlena's right," Taye confirmed, smiling down at Jewel and then at his many relatives who had crowded around. He put an arm around Jewel and possessively held on to her. "This beautiful lady will be back as Caprice, but with a new director, of course."

Cheers of approval erupted and then everyone applauded when Taye placed a lingering kiss on Jewel, letting her and his family know that he planned to permanently share the spotlight with her.

REQUEST YOUR FREE BOOKS!

2 FREE NOVELS PLUS 2 FREE GIFTS!

KIMANI™ ROMANCE

Love's ultimate destination!